SEEING

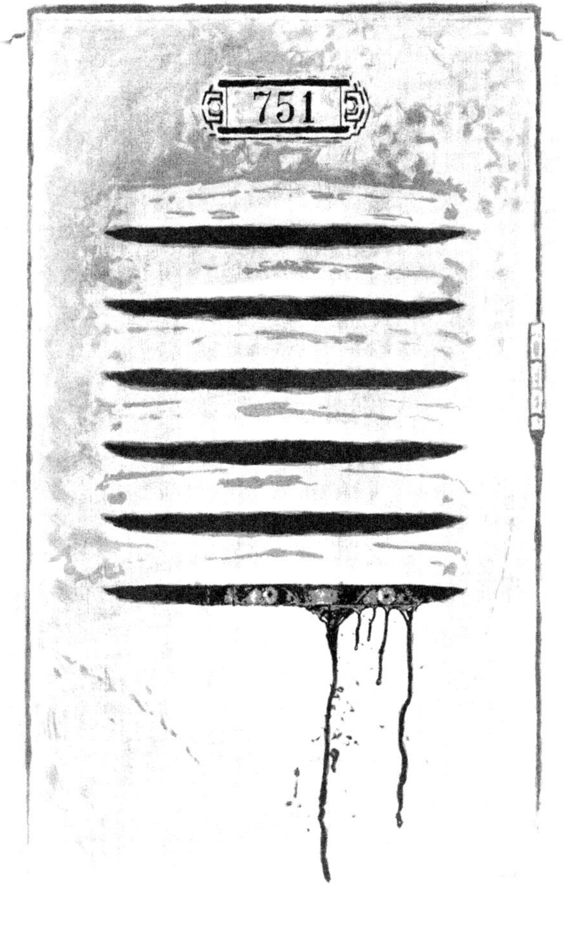

BY SONORA TAYLOR

Seeing Things by Sonora Taylor

© 2020 Sonora Taylor. All rights reserved.

No portion of this book may be reproduced in any form without permission from the author.

For more information, visit the author's website at www.sonorawrites.com

This is a work of fiction. Names, characters, businesses, places, events, and incidents are either the products of the author's imagination or used in a fictitious manner. Any resemblance to actual persons, living or dead, or actual events is purely coincidental.

Cover art by Doug Puller.

For my niece. I love you, Bug.

CHAPTER 1

One thing Abby learned about growing up was that there was a lot of blood involved. She often nicked her knees when she shaved her legs, and one little drop of blood never failed to appear no matter how often she blotted it. The underwire in her new bra, an upgrade from the trainer she'd worn since fifth grade, still poked the sides of her boobs and left welts. And of course, there was her period, which greeted her right before Saint Patrick's Day and about one month after her thirteenth birthday. "Guess you could say it's a rite of spring," her mother said with a cheeky grin as she handed her a pad.

Abby rolled her eyes and slammed the bathroom door. The wooden barrier wasn't enough to block out her mother muttering something about PMS. Abby sighed and stayed in the bathroom. She wished she could curl into the tub and trickle down the drain like blood from her nicked knee.

She didn't, though—she only continued to grow, and still saw blood every month. It got on her sheets and stained her favorite jeans. Abby's sex ed teacher said that periods were nothing to be ashamed of: they were a sign of womanhood, and neither dirty nor embarrassing. Abby scrunched her nose as she shuffled in her seat. She wasn't embarrassed, but her sheets would have a word to say about the blood not being dirty.

As much as she hated it, though, it was blood she'd come to expect. That was more than she could say for the trail of blood she saw in the hallway when she left the classroom.

Abby shrieked and skidded to a halt. Someone collided into her. "Watch it!" a girl named Gina said as she gave her a shove.

"What's going on?" her teacher, Mrs. Yates, called as the other students pushed past Abby.

"Someone's bleeding in the hallway!" Abby cried.

The kids next to her stopped, and Mrs. Yates rushed to the door. "There's nothing there," Gina said with a sneer.

"Are you blind?" Abby spat. She pointed at the three straight lines of blood that ended at the lockers. "Maybe someone cut themselves on the locker door, or—"

"Or maybe they got their period," Gina cracked.

"Gina!" Mrs. Yates said with pursed lips while the other kids laughed. "And Abby," she said, turning to her and keeping her frown in place. "That's not funny. You shouldn't joke about blood in the halls."

"I'm not joking! I'm—" Abby saw more kids pile into the hallway. They walked over the streaks of blood as if nothing were there. Even more confusing was how the blood didn't smear beneath their steps.

"Do you need to see the nurse?" Mrs. Yates asked.

"No. I think it's just shadows or something." Abby stared at the blood on the floor while her classmates walked past her, some snickering as they passed.

Her friend Carmen elbowed her as they walked to their next class. "You seeing things, Abs?"

"I have no idea," Abby replied.

As her next class began, Abby watched the clock. Five, ten, fifteen minutes went by. She raised her hand, and Mr. Consuelos pointed at her. "Can I go to the bathroom?" she asked.

"En español," Mr. Consuelos corrected.

"Puedo ir el baño, por favor?"

"*Al* baño, and yes."

Abby sped out of the room before Mr. Consuelos could rope her into another quick Spanish lesson. She sped past the bathrooms and straight to the lockers.

The floor was clean.

Abby blinked, then closed her eyes and shook her head. She opened them. A spotless floor lay ahead of her.

Her shoulders slumped. On one hand, she was glad no one was actually bleeding and hurt, but on the other, it made her feel as crazy as Gina and her friends likely thought she was. She was about to turn around when a moving stream caught her attention. She looked and saw three trails of blood trickle out of a locker at the other end of the row in front of her.

Abby walked towards the locker as the blood creeped down the hall. She stepped in front of the locker door. She didn't slip on the blood, but she saw it pool against her shoes, the current rerouted by her feet. She stooped down and saw that the blood was seeping through the bottom crack. She pulled a used Kleenex from her pocket, ready to mop it up and prove to Mrs. Yates, or any teacher really, that she wasn't crazy.

A crash against metal sounded near her head. She gasped and jumped back. The locker door rattled with successive booms. Abby heard a gurgled hiss, but no voice.

The knocks ceased. Abby crept back towards the locker, trying to get the best view that she could through the slats while staying as far away as possible.

A shadow passed through the cracks. Abby took another step closer.

A face slammed against the slats. Abby saw pale cheeks, matted hair, and two oozing holes where there had once been eyes. The gurgled hissing started up again, but now, it sounded like a growl.

Abby turned and ran for the principal's office. The sound of the bloody girl's face slamming against the door echoed behind her.

"I need to see Principal Moss!" Abby yelled as she ran into the front office.

Mr. Charles, the receptionist, looked up at her, startled. "Is something wrong?" he asked.

"There's someone inside a locker! Someone who's bleeding!"

"What?" Mr. Charles dialed the principal and asked her to come out as fast as she can. In a few moments, Principal Moss appeared.

"What's going on?" she asked.

"I was walking through the hall," Abby said, "and I saw blood on the floor."

"Blood? Where?"

"Near the lockers! I checked and there was someone inside Locker 751, someone bleeding!"

Both Principal Moss and Mr. Charles frowned, and their alarm vanished. "I thought this was over with," Mr. Charles muttered as he sat back down.

"Over with?" Abby asked. "Do kids get shoved in that locker all the time or something?"

"Miss Gillman," Principal Moss said, "if you keep making up stories about Locker 751, you'll be suspended."

"I'm not making it up!"

"Abby—"

"Come see! Please! I saw her in there, please, just come with me!"

Abby felt tears prick her eyes, and she felt ashamed. Still, they worked in her favor: pity settled into Principal Moss' face. "Okay, let's go take a look," she said.

Abby thought her response still wasn't appropriate for the news that someone was trapped and bleeding inside of a locker, but at least she was going to come and see.

"Abby, please calm down." Principal Moss tried to soothe Abby as Abby tugged her down the hall. "I'm going as fast as I can."

"I don't know how she got in there," Abby said. "But she's bleeding, and there's blood on the floor, and—"

"And we'll check on it." Principal Moss's walkie-talkie beeped. "Yeah," she said. "Send a security guard to the seventh-grade lockers."

"Yes ma'am," a crackled voice replied.

Abby halted when they approached the seventh-grade hall. She was afraid to turn the corner and see more blood. She was relieved, though, to no longer hear the slamming sounds. Maybe the girl had fainted. She hoped the girl wasn't dead.

"Over here," Abby said as they turned the corner. Principal Moss followed her. Abby stopped when she approached the 700 row of lockers. The blood was gone.

Principal Moss collided into her back. "What's wrong?" she asked, only slightly hiding her irritation.

"The blood's gone."

"And you're sure you saw blood?"

"Yes!" Abby sped towards the locker. Principal Moss followed, but Abby swore she heard a small sigh escape her lips. Abby stopped in front of the locker, and saw the sheen of bloody eyes stare through the slats. She was less afraid this time.

"See?" Abby said. But Principal Moss approached with a shaking head.

"Abby, I don't know if you think this is funny—"

"Funny? She's bleeding!"

"Or if some of the older kids told you a story and scared you—"

"I'm thirteen. I'm not scared by ghost stories."

"But there's nothing in Locker 751."

"Problem, ladies?" Abby and Principal Moss turned and saw Officer Ahmed, the head security guard, walk towards them with a smile.

"Officer Ahmed," Principal Moss said as she motioned towards the locker. "Can you open this, please?"

"Yes, please," Abby said as she stepped aside. "There's—"

"Let him see."

Abby pursed her lips and watched impatiently as Officer Ahmed undid the bolt. The locker opened. Jammed inside was a girl around Abby's age. Her eyes were bloody holes, and her skin was purple and green. Her arms bent up towards her face and her knees were in a permanent squat.

Abby stepped back and let out a cry. But she was distracted from a full-on meltdown by Officer Ahmed chuckling and Principal Moss shaking her head. "Is the Legend of 751 making a resurgence?" he said.

"It seems like it," Principal Moss said.

"What legend?" Abby said. "And of course I'm scared—there's a bloody girl with no eyes in there, right there in front of us."

"Abby—"

"Hey!" Abby stomped towards the girl. Though her eyes were holes Abby swore she saw them glare. "Hey," Abby repeated. "Tell them you're here. Say something!"

The girl spun around and turned her back to Abby. She hissed, then slammed her hands against the locker, leaving bloody handprints that vanished as soon as they appeared.

"Abigail." Principal Moss' hands gently touched her shoulders. Officer Ahmed closed the locker. "There's nothing in there."

Abby stared in defeat at Locker 751. The girl inside turned back around and stared through the slats. Abby wondered if the girl was laughing at her from inside. She wondered if the girl was even there.

"Come on," Principal Moss said. "I think you should go home for the day."

———

Abby paced in front of the school while she waited for her mother to pick her up. Officer Ahmed waited with her. "Gotta make sure you make it home safely," he'd said with a smile when Abby tried to insist she could wait alone.

Please, Abby had thought. *He wants to make sure I don't have a meltdown in the parking lot.*

While she waited, she worked on settling her nerves so she wouldn't seem as frightened as Principal Moss likely told her mother she'd been. It didn't help, though, that Abby's general appearance was one of fright. Her hazel eyes were naturally wide, her light brown hair was frizzed and often stood on end against her shoulders and neck, even after a decent combing; and her skinniness made her elbows and knees stick out. Carmen had once joked that Abby looked like a skeleton dancing her way through a year-round Día de los Muertos.

A horn honked twice behind her. Abby jumped and turned around. She saw her mother's purple Camry moving towards her. Abby frowned as she tried to slow her breathing. So much for not looking scared.

Abby walked as slowly as possible towards her mother. She saw her mother staring ahead, but not at her. Her fingers were on her forehead. Abby frowned. Of course her mother was mad at her for interrupting her workday.

Abby knocked on the car door. Her mother looked up, and Abby braced herself for a look of disappointment.

Her mother grinned, waved, and unlocked the door. Abby felt herself darken further. Couldn't her mother react to having to leave her job and pick up her crazy daughter accordingly? Couldn't any of the adults she'd spoken to today act the way she wanted them to?

"Hey Abs," her mother said as Abby opened the door.

"Abby," Abby said. "Abs are muscles."

"Right. You want a different nickname now."

"It's not different, it's—"

"Let's not argue about this now, okay?" Her mother pursed her lips, and Abby slid down in her seat.

They drove out of the parking lot.

"So, your principal said you had a little fright today," her mother said.

"It wasn't little," Abby said.

"I guess crying and getting the principal wouldn't be little." Her mother chuckled. A little voice told Abby her mother was just trying to cheer her up, but Abby was in no mood to pay it heed.

"It's not funny," Abby said.

"I know it isn't. It's also okay to be scared." Her mother squeezed her knee, and Abby closed her eyes. "I got pretty scared too when I heard the Legend of Locker 751."

"I've never heard it, though."

"I mean, you aren't supposed to. They banned kids from telling it after—"

Abby perked up, but her mother pursed her lips. "After what?" she asked.

"After things got out of hand."

Abby slumped in her seat and looked out the window. Her mother almost never wanted to tell her the whole story. She told her she didn't need to be burdened with the problems of grown-ups. Maybe that was necessary when Abby was six, but she was thirteen. She could handle it.

"But maybe you heard it anyway," her mother continued. Keeping the attention on Abby and her craziness, instead of what was really going on with Locker 751. Abby fumed and said nothing.

"Or maybe one of your friends heard it. Carmen's always telling some ghost story. I'm amazed she hasn't scared you to death yet—"

"She only tells *some* ghost stories, and they don't scare me." Carmen's interests were more in true crime and reading about old serial killers, but Abby knew better than to bring that up just then. "And she didn't tell me about Locker 751. No one did. I saw blood, and I followed it to the locker, and a dead girl was inside of it. I didn't even know what locker it was until I saw her eyes."

"There's no one in that locker. Principal Moss looked right at it. You have to believe her, honey, if only for your own sanity."

Abby closed her mouth and looked out the window. Tears pricked her eyes. Her tears came faster than they had when she was younger. Something else she hated about growing up.

"You'd rather believe her than me," Abby said, her voice low so her mother wouldn't hear her choked voice.

A chill settled between them, the one Abby recognized from when she'd managed to strike somewhere deep within her mother's heart, even when she didn't mean to. This time though, it made Abby feel good. She wasn't the only one who was vulnerable.

They drove without speaking the rest of the way home. Abby didn't mind the quiet, even as the tension thickened between them with every mile in silence.

"I believe you saw what you saw," her mother said as they pulled into the garage. "But I also believe your principal."

"You can't believe both of us."

"I can believe you saw something and also believe it wasn't there."

"You think I'm crazy." Abby turned to face her mother as she undid her seatbelt. "You think I'm nuts or making things up or scared of some stupid ghost story. You think this is PMS too or something?"

"PMS? What are you—"

"I'm going to my room." Abby grabbed her backpack as she exited the car, slamming the door right behind her. She hurried to the door and unlocked it with her own keys before her mother caught up with her. She ran up the stairs and retreated to her room, closing the door behind her. She heard her mother come inside, but there were no footsteps in the hall, nor a knock on her door.

Abby turned onto her side and closed her eyes, trying to forget about the girl in Locker 751. Part of her wanted to go downstairs, apologize, and ask for comfort. Instead, she took in the quiet. It was something she did with increasing frequency, in time with her body growing and her thoughts shifting in all sorts of directions. There was a lot of blood involved with growing up, and there was also a lot of loneliness.

CHAPTER 2

Abby stayed in her room. She did her homework, but otherwise stayed on her bed, lost in thought. Why could she see the girl when no one else could? Had anyone ever told her a story about that locker? Eighth graders almost never spoke to her. Gina and her friends picked on Abby in class, but it was about her voice or her shoes or other things that Abby hadn't realized she cared about until they pointed them out. They never talked about ghosts.

A tap on the door broke her concentration. Abby was about to say, "Come in," but stopped herself when she imagined her mother on the other side of the door. She didn't know if she wanted to see her.

"Abby? It's Dad."

Abby dropped her shoulders with relief. "Come in," she said.

Her father walked in and smiled when he saw her. "Hey sweetheart," he said as he sat on the edge of the bed. "Heard you had a rough day at school."

Abby frowned and leaned against her pillow. "You think I'm crazy too?"

"I've known you were crazy since you were a baby." Abby couldn't help but smile as her dad chuckled. "I don't think you're crazy," he said. "And neither does your mom."

Abby sighed a little. "I know."

"Have you been feeling stressed at school, though? Is anything wrong?"

Not until she'd seen the blood in the hallway. "No," Abby said. "But I swear I saw something. There was blood trickling down the hall, and I saw a young girl in there with gouged out eyes and—" Her father flinched, and Abby decided to move on from the violence. "And I don't know what the hell—"

"Language."

"Really? I can't say hell?"

"You'll get unlimited hell privileges when you're in high school."

"Fine." Abby giggled a little as she spoke. "Well, I don't know what the heck everyone was talking about with that locker. Do you know the Legend of 751?"

Her father took a deep breath, like he was about to visit the last place he wanted to go. "Unfortunately, yeah. I was in high school by the time we moved here, so I only heard traces, but your uncle went to middle school around the time the legend was in full swing. We didn't use the Internet as much back in the dinosaur ages of the nineties. We made up our own lies. I know the school's cracked down on kids sharing that story, but lies tend to persist. You probably heard traces of the story."

"No one I know's ever talked about it," Abby insisted.

"Well, it's your typical ghost story. Back in the sixties, a girl went missing. It varies what happened—she was out on a date, she was serving detention, she'd broken into the school to meet up with a boy—but she was gone for two days before someone noticed blood trickling out of her locker."

"Locker 751?"

"Yup. They opened it up and found her body."

Abby scrunched her nose. "That's it?"

Her father laughed, but uncomfortably. "I'd hardly call a corpse 'that's it,'" he said.

"No no, I mean … that's awful, but it doesn't sound like a legend."

"The legend came from other kids claiming they saw her in the locker. They said she haunted it. But they took the locker out of commission when a girl named Laura snapped over it."

Abby grew intrigued. "Snapped? How?"

"Laura kept telling people that she could see the girl. She was friends with your uncle, and was always trying to convince him that there was a ghost. She told the teachers, her friends, everyone. No one believed her, though, because there was nothing in there—it was just a legend. Laura was so convinced that she wanted to hold a séance outside the locker."

Abby wrinkled her brow at the image of candles and a girl chanting outside of the locker. She hoped she'd never look as silly as that.

"But it didn't work, and she felt so alone that she had a breakdown. She gouged her eyes out so she wouldn't see the girl anymore, and died from her wounds."

"Gouged her eyes? Like the girl who was killed?"

"Yes, just like the girl. Another part of the story." Her father looked at her sorrowfully. "A part that Laura took on herself because she was so convinced she'd seen something."

Abby was so relieved to have her father tell her more—something her mother hadn't trusted Abby enough to do herself—that she didn't mind that her father didn't believe her.

"It's okay to get scared," her dad continued. "And it's okay to have an imagination. But if it's going to make you scared and afraid and act out at school, then we can't have that. I don't want what happened to Laura to happen to you."

Abby grew ashamed at having worried her father. She didn't want him to occupy himself with what he thought was her imagination. Maybe it was her imagination.

"It won't," Abby assured him. "I won't. I won't hurt myself, I mean. Maybe—maybe it was something I ate."

It sounded weak before it'd even left her mouth, but it seemed good enough for her father. "And I'm sorry about what I said to Mom," Abby said. "Did she tell you what—"

"She didn't say anything except that you had a rough day at school and that you thought you saw something scary."

"Well, tell her I'm sorry."

"Tell her yourself. It's almost dinnertime."

CHAPTER 3

Abby hugged her mother in the kitchen before sitting down for dinner. She didn't say sorry, but her mother didn't ask her to. Her remorse passed between them, and Abby sensed her mother could more strongly feel it in her bones than hear it in her ears. She and her parents talked about anything but school while they ate. She finished her homework and went to bed.

The next morning, the phone rang. Abby looked up from her cereal as her parents looked at it in surprise. "Can you get it, David?" her mother asked, since she was in the middle of preparing her own breakfast.

"Can't. You know there's always traffic on the way into the office," her father said as he chugged his coffee. He bolted out of the kitchen. The phone rang again, and Abby heard her mother sigh in frustration before picking it up.

"Hello?" she said curtly. Her face softened. "Oh, hello." Abby furrowed her eyebrows as her mother listened. "Yes, Abby's fine. I think she just got scared."

Abby figured it was Principal Moss. She hoped that her episode the day before was only known to Principal Moss, Officer Ahmed, and Mr. Charles. Even that was three people too many for her liking. She stared at her cereal and took a big bite to try and focus on anything else.

"I do think she's fine," her mother continued. "Her father talked to her, and she's been in good spirits since. I don't think she needs anything else. She'll be in school today."

Abby looked up again. Anything else? Like what?

"Thank you, Mrs. Moss." Her mother hung up the phone and returned to making her breakfast.

"What did Principal Moss think I need?" Abby asked.

"Nothing you need just yet," her mother assured her. "But if you have a scare like that again, let us know, okay sweetheart? Then maybe we can talk to a doctor or something."

Abby paused mid-chew. Her mother held up her hand in assurance. "Nothing extreme, and nothing just yet. But you were really scared yesterday."

"I was. But I'm fine now." Abby returned to her cereal and didn't look at her mother, even when she heard her sigh again—this time, with sadness.

———

Abby rode the bus with a bit of trepidation. She wasn't afraid of Locker 751. A small part of her hoped she wouldn't see the streaks or the ghost, but even if she did, she'd dismiss them. It wasn't worth the worry and judgment from the adults in her life, not to mention the doctor's appointments that could come from Abby seeing things in the hallway.

What she was more worried about was being tortured by her classmates. She was grateful that they'd all been in class when she'd seen the girl in the locker. Still, word travelled fast through middle school halls, especially when someone left school early. Abby hoped they all thought she'd just been sick.

Abby sat down in homeroom. Carmen walked in shortly after. Her eyes brightened when she saw Abby at her desk. "Where were you yesterday?" Carmen asked. "I had to suffer through Pre-Algebra all by myself."

"Sorry," Abby said. "I got sick on my way to the bathroom yesterday and went home early."

"You seem fine now."

"Just a daylong bug."

"Well, Mr. DiMartinez made us all suffer. We had a pop quiz yesterday!" Carmen went on about the horrors of math class until the bell rang. Abby's classes went remarkably well, in terms of her classmates asking about the day before. They only asked where she'd been, if they asked her anything at all.

It was only at lunch that Abby's relief began to fade. "Watch out, Abby!" Gina said as she walked by their lunch table. She pointed towards a smear on the tile near the trash can. "There's blood on the floor!"

"Bitch, that's ketchup," her friend Stacy said with an eye roll.

"I know, stupid, it's a joke!" Gina and Stacy squabbled with each other as they continued past Abby's table, the snickers of the rest of Gina's group the only trace of teasing left behind.

"Just ignore them," Carmen said, even though Abby was doing that already. "They'll forget all about it by tomorrow."

"Right." Abby didn't like being teased, but she'd take a joke about the blood over jokes about the girl in the locker.

"Think about summer instead. Just around the corner!"

"I know, it's gonna be awesome."

"You still going to your uncle and aunt's?" Carmen asked.

"Yeah. Uncle Keith and Aunt Sandra are fixing up Grandma and Grandpa's old house, and I'm going to help them."

"What's their house like?"

"I've never been."

"Oh right, yeah—never met your grandparents." Carmen snickered as she bit into a baby carrot. "I can't imagine what your life is like, with just your parents and an aunt and uncle that are never here. During the holidays, I can't spit without hitting el abuelito or la tía or un primo somewhere in our house. And they think *our* family's small because it's just me and Hector!"

"Well, we're pretty tight-knit." As close as Abby was with Carmen, she preferred not to talk about how much her father actively avoided talking about his parents. Abby had never met them, and had only seen their photograph once. She was five, and had been exploring her parent's bedroom. It sat in a frame surrounded by old sheriff's badges that said "David Gillman." When Abby asked her mother when her dad had been a sheriff, her mother said the badges were her grandfather's—they shared a first name—before scolding her for going through their things.

While she didn't know much about them, Abby knew that they were people her father visited. He'd disappear once or twice a month to go to their retirement home, which was just outside her hometown of Phillip's Glen. She asked him once if she could go with him, and he gave her a stern no. When she asked why, he narrowed his eyes, and Abby could sense "because I said so" behind his expression.

He'd softened though, and said, "I see them because I'm their son. Your grandparents are big on the things you have to do, especially for family and for appearances. I don't expect you to feel the same way—and I don't really want them to be in your life. They're not the nicest people."

"But I'm their family, right?" Abby asked.

"Right, but that doesn't mean you have to be around people like your grandparents, not when you don't have to."

"Do you have to?"

"Kind of, yeah. But you don't, and you should be grateful. Focus on the family you have: me, your mom, her parents—"

"They're coming for Christmas this year, right?"

"Or course! And focus on Uncle Keith."

Uncle Keith never saw his parents either. Even after Abby's grandparents died, he stayed put in Sangway Bluff, where he'd moved to teach before Abby was born. He never came to visit Abby and her parents. They were always welcome to visit him, though; and when Abby came to see him, he always pointed out the house they'd all lived in before moving away from the coast.

That was the house on the beach that needed fixing up. "I'm looking forward to seeing where Dad and Uncle Keith lived as kids," Abby told Carmen. "Apparently the house is really old."

"Think they'll let you write down all the work you're going to do for your community service next year?"

"Even if they didn't, I'd want to go. I haven't been to Sangway Bluff in years." The last time Abby had visited her aunt and uncle, she had been nine years old. Before that, she'd gone every summer for a month-long visit. Aunt Sandra would take her to the counseling center where she worked some days and let her color; and they would ride bikes in the woods near their apartment building.

Uncle Keith was an English teacher, and since he had summer vacation as well, they would spend more time together. He'd often slipped her books with a wink as he said, "Read this. I know your teachers won't assign it." Abby always thought she'd get to read something dark and forbidden, but it was usually just a book that had come out in the past five years. She admitted that still fit the criteria of something that wasn't very likely to be assigned by her teachers.

He would also drive them to the beach where he and Abby's father had grown up and take her for rides on his speed boat around the coast. When she was really little, he'd played his guitar and sung to her before she went to sleep. She'd asked him if he was a rock star, and Aunt Sandra had said, "In his mind." Both Aunt Sandra and Uncle Keith laughed, but he'd been a rock star in Abby's mind too.

The summer she was ten, though, she hadn't packed her bags for Sangway Bluff. Uncle Keith and Aunt Sandra were going on a two-week long cruise, her mother explained. They would return too close to their own planned family vacation for Abby to be able to go. Her father had muttered something about the two of them needing more than a cruise to fix things between them, but her mother shot him a dirty look before Abby could ask him to explain.

When Abby was eleven, her father suggested she could stay at home during the day while they were at work over the summer—there was no need for Uncle Keith and Aunt Sandra to babysit Abby for a month. Abby hadn't thought that her aunt and uncle considered her visits babysitting, and in her embarrassment, she'd agreed.

Visiting her aunt and uncle hadn't even come up when she was twelve. It seemed her visits to Sangway Bluff would become a childhood memory, to fade in time along with what it felt like to not have to wear a bra every day.

That year though, during her birthday call, Uncle Keith told Abby that over the summer, he and Aunt Sandra would be fixing up her grandparents' old beach house. "We'll be on the coast, where I used to take you boating, remember?"

"Yeah. You still have the boat?"

"You bet. But your aunt and I were thinking you could come help us, if you'd like to come visit."

Abby perked up immediately at the thought of returning to Sangway Bluff. "You want me to come?" she asked.

"Of course we do! I haven't seen you in ages. I miss you, Skipper."

Abby's heart warmed at hearing her nickname, which Uncle Keith had given her based on some show about an island he'd said his parents watched, because of all the boating they did together. But she especially loved that she'd been missed. At a time when she felt like she was in everyone's way, it was nice to be wanted.

"You'll have to ask your parents, of course, but—"

"I want to come. I'll ask them." And to Abby's delight, they'd readily agreed. She'd be back in Sangway Bluff, back with her aunt and uncle, and back to everything she missed.

The lunch bell rang. "Well, make sure you text me over the summer when you're in Sangway Bluff," Carmen said as they gathered up their trays.

"I will," Abby promised. She began to follow Carmen towards the trash can, when she skidded to a stop. Another student stood right in her path.

"Hey, watch out," Abby said as she jerked back her tray.

"I'm way ahead of you," Carmen called.

"Not you, him." Abby's eyes widened, though, when she saw other students walk past the boy. He glowered at her, then walked by. The motion felt like an early autumn breeze against her arm.

"Wait!" she called. "Who are you?"

The boy emphatically turned his head and walked away.

"Who ran into you?" Carmen asked.

"I don't know," Abby said as she watched the boy disappear.

Abby decided to take the long way home when she left school. It was about a thirty-minute walk. Her parents had told her she was old enough to walk by herself if she wanted, but she usually preferred riding the bus with Carmen.

She wanted to walk home that afternoon, though, because the route took her past a graveyard.

Abby was already certain that she'd seen the murder victim her father told her about in Locker 751. No one could be alive with all those wounds. The boy in the cafeteria may have been a surly student that no one else had noticed, but that would make two people that Abby could see that others couldn't. And she couldn't forget the chill she felt when the boy had walked by.

Seeing the dead wasn't something that she thought would come with growing up. Maybe, though, it was something else to go along with all the blood.

Abby pushed the gate open and heard it creak with neglect. She never saw anyone working in the cemetery. She wondered who kept the headstones clean and the trails cleared. Did they work at night? Maybe at dusk? Were they afraid of ghosts? Abby shook her head—if they were afraid of ghosts, why would they work in a cemetery?

Abby realized she was getting lost in questions to herself again, which meant she wasn't scanning the grass or the stones for anyone who looked like they should've moved on by now. She fixed her gaze and her thoughts on the cemetery. She stopped when she saw a woman walking up the hill. The woman caught her eye and waved to her.

Abby grinned and felt excitement at the dead talking to her, when she realized the woman was very much alive. Her skin was healthy, her clothes were clean, and she held a bouquet of flowers. She was here to mourn the dead, not look for them.

Abby continued, grateful she'd caught on before she'd asked the woman if she was dead. How would she ask that? They wouldn't all be bloody like the girl in the locker. They may be cold like the boy in the cafeteria, but would she have to walk up to everyone she suspected was dead and see if she felt that same chill? She hated approaching people she didn't know as it was. There was no way she wanted to get close to people to see if they passed some sort of dead test.

Abby continued walking the path. The cemetery was small, and she finished in under an hour. There was no sign of anyone else, living or dead. Abby sighed when she returned to the gate. She supposed the only way she'd know if she'd seen a dead person was if she had the shit scared out of her at school—and even then, that wasn't proof of anything except that she was seeing things.

Abby kept her eyes low as she walked down the sidewalk. She approached a pair of tattered shoes. The person who owned them made slow, quiet footsteps. "Excuse me," she said in a quiet voice.

The person turned. The first thing Abby noticed was that he wore some sort of formal suit, even though it was June. It was frayed at the cuffs of his sleeves and his pants alike. His hair was smooth and black like the men in silent films they'd watched in her mass media class, and his eyes had a similar, sallow-looking shadow beneath them.

It was his face, though, that made Abby gasp. Abby had seen him before, in a different class. He was James Holden, the youngest mayor of Phillip's Glen. In history class they'd learned that he'd also been the first mayor when the town was founded in 1903—and a short-lived mayor, after he'd hung himself one year into his term. The man in front of her was dead, dead, dead—and Abby could see him.

Further, he could see and hear her. He'd turned to face her, and now, he stared at her. His neutral look, though, quickly vanished when they made eye contact. His eyes narrowed, and then he pivoted and hurried down the street.

"Wait!" Abby called. She chased after him, looking side to side to see if anyone was nearby. Even if she could see Mayor Holden, she knew that no one else could; and she didn't want to look like a crazy person yelling at an invisible, dead mayor in the middle of town. But she wasn't crazy—she was psychic. Or was it gifted? Or clairvoyant? Maybe just able to see ghosts? Whatever she was, she was real, and so were the people she could see.

The people she saw, though, didn't seem to want to see her. Mayor Holden dashed around another corner, and Abby picked up her pace. "Why are you here?" she called. "Why can I see you? Do you want to tell me something?"

Mayor Holden stopped and turned. He glared at her, but Abby felt excitement all the same. She had a gift, a purpose. Something that didn't weigh on her like bras or pads or self-esteem. Something she could use and something unique—and now, Mayor Holden had a message for her.

The message was brief. Mayor Holden jerked up his hand, middle finger raised. He turned and disappeared down another street. Abby was too stunned to follow him.

"Wow," she breathed once she collected herself. "Dick!"

CHAPTER 4

Abby walked home feeling worse than when she'd seen the girl in Locker 751. It was one thing for school officials to think she was nuts, or her parents to think she was imagining things. It was another thing entirely to be despised by people she'd never even met.

Even if they weren't as rude as Mayor Holden and his gesture, Abby knew that the other dead people she'd seen had hated her. The boy in the cafeteria glared at her and walked right by. The girl in the locker turned her back to Abby.

It hurt. She didn't even know any of them—she only knew Mayor Holden because of a history lesson. What did they have against her?

It wasn't so much their hatred for her—Abby wasn't about to take the opinions of ghosts too seriously—but for the complete lack of sense that her gift made if she was so reviled. Why did she have the ability to see and talk to the dead if none of them wanted to talk to her? If she was going to be caught off guard by the sight of people no one else could see, she at least wanted something better out of it than being startled by the sudden appearance of ghosts, only to then be insulted and ignored by all of them.

Abby shook off her disappointment as she walked up her steps. She wouldn't think about them now. She had a vacation in Sangway Bluff to prepare for. She brightened at the thought of seeing Uncle Keith, Aunt Sandra, and the beach.

Abby opened the door and was about to announce she was home when she heard her parents talking in the kitchen. "I'm just so tired of this!" her father snapped.

Abby closed the door as quietly as she could. She didn't want to interrupt them if they were fighting. She moved towards the stairs when she heard her mother say, "David, please—"

"I'm tired of feeling like Keith's goddamn babysitter."

Abby halted when she heard her uncle's name. She sat on the stairs and stayed as quiet as she could so she could listen to her parents speak.

"He isn't asking you to babysit him," her mother said.

"I just feel like I grew up and he's still acting like the little brother, tripping and crying when I'm not there to pick him up. I mean, what the hell, Denise? First, he's just now fixing up Mom and Dad's old place even though it hasn't had tenants in years—"

"Didn't he have other things to work on?"

"Yeah. His relationship. Which fell apart anyway." Her father snorted, but Abby felt her heart stop.

"You've been busy here with me and Abby. Just because he doesn't have children doesn't mean he has all the time in the world."

"But he had more time than me. He just expected me to pick it up for him or kick his ass into doing it, like always. He's only working on the house now because he needs something to take his mind off Sandra and being unemployed. Unemployed!" Her father slammed his hand on the table. "Jesus Christ, no job and a dead relationship. What's he going to do next, demolish the house?"

"Why don't you show him a little compassion? You think it was easy for him to call you and tell you everything that's going on?"

"Of course it was. It means he can get the whole summer to himself. He probably won't even touch that house."

Uncle Keith wouldn't have the summer to himself: Abby would be there. A chill coursed through Abby's skin. Unless—

Abby sped towards the kitchen. "What happened?" she called so as to announce her presence.

"Abby?" Her father looked up as she entered the kitchen. He sat at the table while her mother, flustered, kept her hands busy with dinner prep. "How long have you been home?"

"What happened to Uncle Keith?"

"Abby, you know better than to listen in on us," her mother said with a frown.

"Am I still going to Sangway Bluff?"

"Uncle Keith lost his job today," her father explained. He motioned to an empty chair at the table, but Abby didn't want to sit. The fear of missing out on Sangway Bluff and not visiting her uncle coursed through her in a panicked adrenaline that kept her on her feet. "Well, he told me today. Yesterday was his last day."

"He quit?"

"No, the principal thought it'd be a good idea for him to leave. Said something about the pressures of teaching becoming too much for him. It was getting to him and affecting his work with the students." Her father snorted. "The man teaches high school English, then plays guitar and drives a boat on weekends. He wants to talk pressure, he should talk to me about my job and all the meetings, traffic, office crap—"

"David," her mother warned.

"Is he your brother, or mine?" her father snapped.

Abby paled. Her mother looked back down at the vegetables.

To her father's credit, he softened immediately. "I'm sorry, honey," he said.

Her mother raised a hand to signal it was fine, though her pursed lips assured them all that it was not.

Her father turned back to Abby. "Uncle Keith's going through a lot, though. He and Aunt Sandra—well, they've been having trouble for a while, and she moved out this morning."

"Isn't she always threatening to break up with him, like a joke?" Abby asked. Aunt Sandra and Uncle Keith both would tease each other about leaving for good, especially when they bickered; but Abby always saw it as playful. Of course, she hadn't seen either of them in almost four years.

"Those weren't always jokes before," her mother said. "They broke up—"

"But got back together—"

"Not this time," her father said. "It's for good. She's moved out and moved to another town."

Gone. Aunt Sandra was gone. No more counseling center, no more poems and no more of her famous sun tea. Abby wondered if she'd ever see her again. She also thought about how sad Uncle Keith must be. Everything was gone: his job, his parents, his girlfriend, even his brother, in a way.

But his niece wouldn't be. "I'll be sure to be extra nice to him when I go visit," Abby said.

Both her parents hesitated, and Abby grew cold. "I'm still going, right?"

"We don't know," her father said.

Abby saw the summer she'd envisioned crashing before her eyes. No beach, no boats, no Uncle Keith. A lump formed in her throat, and her cheeks grew hot.

"It may be too much for Uncle Keith to handle right now," her father continued. "With Sandra being gone and him having to find a new job, he doesn't need to be babysitting—"

"He wouldn't be babysitting me," Abby spat. "I'm thirteen years old. I can watch myself during the day."

"Maybe that wasn't the right word," her father conceded. "But he'd still be responsible for you, and by himself."

"I can take care of myself. And I can help Uncle Keith with the house, so he won't have to leave it alone all summer. I'll help him out and keep him company."

"I don't know if you should be spending the summer alone with a grown man," her mother said.

Abby looked at her mother in disbelief. "He's my uncle, not a stranger."

"It would still be awkward, honey."

"I've spent time alone with him before, like on his boat or when Aunt Sandra would spend a weekend with her sisters in Connecticut." Uncle Keith had called those times the official meetings of the Gillman Crew. It made her feel like she and Uncle Keith were in a secret club, one that she'd been welcomed into as opposed to someone being forced to let her join.

"That was different," her mother said. "You weren't thirteen years old."

"Denise, come on," her father interjected. "Keith's many things, but he's not a child molester."

Her mother threw her hands up and said, "Well, when someone's fired from their teaching job around teenagers and won't tell us the reason outright, it makes me wonder why."

"So you automatically think he's a perv?"

"Just like you automatically think he's lazy."

"He's none of those things!" Abby cried, if only to get her parents to stop arguing. Her father put his head in his hands.

"Whatever he is, he only seems to make things worse between us," he said.

It wasn't Uncle Keith doing that, though—it was everything her mother and father were assuming about him. Abby widened her eyes at the thought. She was surprised by its ugliness toward her parents and yet certain of its truth—and only slightly uncertain that she shouldn't say it out loud.

"I'm going upstairs," Abby said in a low voice. Her parents didn't try to stop her. She hung her head as she closed the door and sat on her bed. She played Candy Crush to try and take her mind off of everything going on. It proved futile, though, as she thought so much about Sangway Bluff that she could barely discern the rows of candy. She pressed her phone face down on the bed and closed her eyes.

The phone chimed. Abby sighed as she checked it. She hoped Carmen had found some new serial killer legend or dirty joke to cheer her up.

It was Uncle Keith. Abby raised her eyebrows. He usually only texted her to say happy birthday or merry Christmas—something quick and impersonal.

Hey Skipper—you home from school? he'd asked.

Abby swallowed the lump in her throat, convinced he'd be able to detect her tears through her typed words. *Yeah. Talked to Mom and Dad. I'm sorry.* She hoped it wasn't too awkward to say so.

She saw three dots signaling Uncle Keith's reply. The dots disappeared without a message, and Abby figured she'd either said the wrong thing or, at best, he didn't want to talk about it.

A moment later, though, her screen turned black as she saw an incoming call from Uncle Keith.

Abby normally preferred text, but given everything that was happening to him, she figured Uncle Keith wouldn't want to be denied a call. "Hey," she said with a voice that was thankfully steady.

"Hey Abby." Her uncle's voice immediately brought his full image to her mind. She imagined him sitting at the kitchen table, but leaning back as if he were in a recliner. His long legs would be all the way past the other side of the table, and probably in jeans and the same pair of boots he'd had since college; and which he always wore inside no matter how many times Aunt Sandra told him not to. His free hand would be running through his mop of soft curls—Abby had called them muddy sand dunes when she was little, since his wavy brown hair reminded her of the beach, but Uncle Keith had said he'd rather not be compared to mud. He'd spoken with a chuckle, as he often did; but that evening his voice sounded tired and resigned.

"So," Uncle Keith continued. "You know all about my problems, huh?"

"I'm sorry," Abby repeated.

"I am too. Seems a lot of my mistakes are catching up with me. So, almost done with school for the year, right?" His voice changed abruptly. It was higher and yet seemed to be tiptoeing around what was happening in his life. Abby recognized that tone from when her parents wanted to change the subject. It normally drove her crazy, but she decided not to fight him on it.

"Yeah," she replied.

"You starting high school next year?"

"Eighth grade."

"Right, right. I missed a year. Probably because you're so smart." He chuckled in a way that told Abby he was making fun of himself, not patronizing her; and for that she was grateful. She smiled. It was small, but it was also the first time she'd smiled since she'd been to the graveyard. It had been awhile since she'd visited Uncle Keith, but she remembered enough to know that he had a knack for making her feel better.

"I want to talk about this summer," Abby said. "I know you've got a lot going on, but—I still want to visit you, if that's okay."

"Oh yeah, of course!" Abby felt immense relief at how quickly her uncle had agreed. Like their weekends as the

Gillman Crew, it made her feel like he wanted her there, as opposed to just watching her to give her parents a break. "We're gonna have our work cut out for us with the house, though."

"I can do it."

"I'm sure you can. You still want to come, right?"

"I do, it's just that Mom and Dad said they didn't know if that was still happening, what with everything going on."

"Well, I'm good with it if you are—"

"I am."

"—and if your parents are too."

That Abby wasn't sure about. She realized too late that her silence revealed that to Uncle Keith, for he sighed a little into the phone. "Your mom and dad are probably just worried about overwhelming me. I'll call them, okay?"

Abby remembered how furious her dad had been after Uncle Keith's last call, and wasn't sure that was a good idea. "I can ask them," Abby offered.

"You can, but I need to tell them it's alright. I want to see you, though. It's been way too long, and I'm sorry about that."

It had, and it'd been because of her parents. Abby darkened at that thought, and further at the idea that they'd keep her from visiting him yet again. "It's not your fault," Abby said.

"I could've been better about including time with you the past four summers, or even getting my ass down to Phillip's Glen—sorry, my butt down to Phillip's Glen—"

"I'm thirteen, you can say 'ass' around me."

"Well, don't tell your dad, and I won't tell him you just said it."

"I was quoting you!"

"A fine excuse, but no dice with your folks if I recall correctly." Uncle Keith chuckled, and Abby smiled once again. "But if all this crap's shown me anything, it's pushed me to get my priorities in order, and I'm going to start by being more present. I promise."

"I believe you."

"Good. Well, I better get off the phone with you so I can get on the phone with your parents. I love you, sweetie."

"Love you too, Uncle Keith. See you in a couple weeks." She hoped that saying it would make it so.

CHAPTER 5

Uncle Keith called Abby's parents after dinner. Abby was dying to listen in as her father spoke to him, but she knew better than to test his patience. The temptation only grew when he went straight to her mother to talk in their room.

It was agreed that Abby would go, but for a week. "Uncle Keith may not know it, but he needs some time to be alone and clear his head," her father told her.

"But it'll also be good for you to see each other," her mother said.

Even with just a week as opposed to the summer, Abby was ecstatic. She spent the rest of the time between the last day of school and her visit thinking about Sangway Bluff. She imagined riding in Uncle Keith's boat, riding past the islands off the coast, exploring her father and uncle's old house, getting a lobster roll on the wharf, all of it. She was sorry that Aunt Sandra wouldn't be there, but seeing Uncle Keith again was good enough for her.

Abby and her parents left for Sangway Bluff on a sunny Sunday morning. Abby watched with glee as the painted row houses and asphalt-covered hills of Phillip's Glen disappeared in favor of rocky cliffs, dunes, and the ocean.

After two-and-a-half hours of driving, with no stops per her father's insistence, they arrived. Abby got out of the car, grateful to be able to stretch her legs. As she arched her back, her eyes wandered to the sand leading up to her grandparents' house. She jumped mid-stretch. Four jagged streaks of blood ran from the bottom of the house to the grass. They seemed to be trickling from somewhere beneath the house.

"What's up, Abs—I'm sorry, Abby." Her mother chuckled as she walked towards Abby. Abby knew better than to tell her what was actually up, so she tried to settle her startled expression.

Her mother smiled and patted her back. "Are you looking at the red sand?" she asked.

Abby felt a mixture of amazement and relief. "You see them too?"

"Of course I do." Her mother stooped down and picked up a clump of sand—sand which was clean, and nowhere near the streaks that Abby saw crawling from the house. "It's volcanic," her mother explained as she let it sift from her fingers back to the ground. "Broken-down lava rocks. You usually only see red sand like this up in PEI, but some of it made its way here, I guess." Her mother rubbed her hands together, and flecks of sand moved from her palms and fingers to the ground. "Make sure you walk barefoot on it. I swear it has restorative properties."

"Will do," Abby said. She hoped her mother couldn't hear her disappointment. Abby looked away from the blood, which definitely wasn't red sand. The blood was a series of dark maroon streaks cutting through what Abby now noticed was a blend of typical tan sand and a rusty-colored grain. Instead she focused on her grandparents' house. It reminded Abby of the older library books she saw in the back aisles, its white wooden sides yellowed with age and its book-cover roof warped from both wind and sun. Forest green windowsills added some life to the place, but they too had fallen victim to age and saltwater breezes. They looked like dried sheets of seaweed, the only extra color coming from splotches of seagull poop splattered against the slats. The house stood on a small bluff away from the tide, but its height over the beach gave it a lopsided appearance, as if the bluff was in league with the ocean and would soon cash in on their deal to topple the structure into the water with the next full tide.

Still, there was an antique beauty to the place. It sat on a cluster of grass and reeds, and the hill leading down from the house—the streaks of blood notwithstanding—had an assortment of tiny shells dotting the sand that led to the smoother surfaces of the beach. The ocean was close enough to be visible from the porch and most every window, yet far enough away to feel like the house was its own private quarters, separated from laughing tourists and hungry birds looking for fish. Abby could see why Uncle Keith wanted to spend the summer trying to save it—and why her father was annoyed that it had been ignored for so long.

"You'd think he'd have at least power washed the windows," her father muttered as they walked up to the front door. He stopped grumbling the minute her mother gave him a look, one that even Abby felt the fury of.

Abby's father knocked on the door. The sound tied a knot in Abby's stomach. Ever since her birthday, she'd been excited to see Uncle Keith. But it had been four years. What if he was nothing like she remembered? What if the voice she'd heard on the phone was the only part of him that rang familiar when she saw him again? She took a breath to try and calm herself, but the sound of Uncle Keith's footsteps coming towards the door tightened the knot a little more with each step.

The door opened, and the knot in her stomach unraveled in time with the creak of the hinge. It was Uncle Keith, mostly as she remembered. His hair had wisps of grey swirling through the curls, his eyes and mouth had a few stray lines beside them, and his skin seemed a little more weathered; but it was him—and he seemed as happy to see them as she was to see him.

"Hey!" he said as he stepped onto the porch. He went towards Abby's father. She looked and saw with relief that her father's earlier sour mood had vanished.

"Long time no see," her father said as they embraced. The hug was brief and ended with a slap on the back. Abby wondered why men couldn't hug each other without slapping each other afterward. "Good to see you, man."

"Likewise." Uncle Keith moved towards her mom, who also leaned in for a brief hug. "Denise, good to see you," he said as her mother patted his arms.

"You too," she replied. "How are you?"

But Uncle Keith had already separated from Abby's mom. His attention moved to Abby, who did her best to smile despite the look of shock that crossed his face.

"Jesus. You never know how long it's been until you see someone growing up." He stooped down—though not as much as he'd had to when she was little—and held out his arms. Abby moved in, and he gave her a tighter hug than her mother or father combined. Abby smelled his scent, a mixture of cloves and saltwater. It was just as she remembered.

"How've you been, Skipper?" he asked as he pulled away, though he kept his hands on her shoulders. "Christ, you're getting tall."

"Let's check Abby's height inside," her father said as he motioned towards the door. "I need your bathroom."

"Right, right. Come on in." They walked inside. Abby's father darted towards the bathroom, and Abby looked at the hallway leading to a kitchen and a living room. If must were a color, the walls and floor were bathed in it. There was no carpet, no brightly-colored wallpaper, no pictures or décor. Even the curtains were a basic, flimsy white that seemed to sigh as the ocean breeze blew through them.

"Cheery, huh?" Uncle Keith said. Abby turned to face him, and saw a small smile on his face. "It's amazing what years of nothing will do to a place."

"You've had a lot on your plate," her mother said.

Uncle Keith paused, then looked down and nodded once. "Yeah," he said. "It's been rough."

Abby wondered if it'd be okay to hug him again. Before she could decide, he looked up with a trace of the smile he'd had before. "But working on the house'll get my mind off things—not to mention catching up with Abby." He grinned at her, and Abby smiled back.

"And you're sure it's not too much?" her mother asked. Abby's skin ran cold. There was no way she'd change her mind and take Abby back, not after the drive here and all their plans—

"Of course not," Uncle Keith said with a wave of his hand, one that seemed to cast a calming spell on Abby's heart. "We'll have a good visit, right Skipper?"

"Right," Abby agreed, even as the empty house stared back at her forlornly.

Abby's father returned, and they gathered in the kitchen. Uncle Keith and her dad sat at the table. Before Abby could join them, her mother said, "Why don't you get your bag and take it to your room?"

Abby was about to protest, as she wanted to visit with everyone first; but Uncle Keith said, "It's the first room on the right when you go upstairs. Probably the only bedroom that doesn't look condemned."

Abby wondered why she was being shoved away so quickly, but as Uncle Keith started talking to her dad, she figured his brother took priority over his niece. She left the kitchen, retrieved her bag from the hall, and headed up steps that let out a screech with every footfall.

Five doors greeted Abby at the top of the stairs. She set her suitcase by the first door on the right and wandered towards the other four rooms. One was a bathroom with a deep, ancient tub with clawed feet. It sat away from the wall and had a copper faucet. Abby wished she'd brought some bath bombs with her, even if the tub was offset by ugly wintergreen walls. Maybe her first task would be to repaint the bathroom.

She continued on, paying little attention to the faded striped wallpaper that was speckled with tiny bits of peeled tatter. One room was filled with so much junk that Abby couldn't discern its previous use. Another was empty save for an antique dresser—Abby figured it had been a bedroom. She wondered whose it had been when her grandparents lived there, Uncle Keith's or her father's. There were no posters, no toys, no indication of whose it could be except that it was small and likely belonged to a child.

If it had belonged to Uncle Keith, it wasn't his bedroom anymore. Abby walked by what appeared to be the master bedroom and saw clutter that indicated it was very much being lived in. Several pieces of dirty laundry lay like bread crumbs in a path towards the hamper, a dresser against the wall held some photos and a watch, a guitar case lay on the floor , and a large four-poster bed—one that looked big enough for three people—lay unmade with a rumpled blue comforter wrinkled over a gigantic mattress. The child in Abby thought of how fun it would be to jump on that bed, but even more so—especially after the drive there—she thought of how comfortable that bed would be for a nap. It was so quiet upstairs. She couldn't even hear her parents' voices from the kitchen. All she heard was the ocean through the window. Abby imagined that sleeping in here brought a sense of peace that the disarray before her didn't match.

Abby returned to her room. She knew it wouldn't be as nice as the master, but she'd long ago accepted that adults always got the nice rooms. While she knew Uncle Keith wouldn't put her in a room as cluttered as the one across the hall, she was still pleasantly surprised to see a tidy guest room waiting for her. A single twin bed sat by an open window. An old teddy bear sat on the pillow, and before she could wrinkle her nose at Uncle Keith thinking she still slept with stuffed animals, she remembered that it was Brigsby, an old toy he'd given her in desperation when she woke up from a nightmare and couldn't be consoled. "He helped me get through some pretty bad nights," Uncle Keith had said as Abby took the bear. "Maybe he'll help you too." Abby wouldn't hold Brigsby to her chest anymore, but she left him on his place of honor on the pillow.

The room had a dresser and a small closet. Abby also saw a bookshelf with one row of books. Of course Uncle Keith would've left her a small library of recommended reading. She smiled at the sight of it.

The quiet that permeated the upstairs rooms filled her room as well. Abby closed her eyes and imagined falling asleep to the sound of the waves. She opened them and looked outside at the beach. The sand was still, and the ocean roared in the distance as a woman in a baseball cap took a late afternoon stroll. Everything about the scene was peaceful, and the tranquility extended to Abby. She felt better than she had in weeks. She was glad her parents had let her come.

———

Abby heard her father and uncle in full conversation when she walked towards the kitchen. She entered with caution in case they still wanted their adults-only time.

"Well, it sounds like you've got your summer mapped out," Abby heard her father say, though she wasn't sure if he sounded convinced or pleased.

"Pretty much," Uncle Keith said with a shrug and a smile. He made eye contact with Abby, and he smiled further. "It'll also help to have someone helping me out around here." Uncle Keith motioned to the only empty chair, and Abby took a seat beside him. "You find your room okay?"

"Yeah," Abby said. "And Brigsby. I'd almost forgotten about him."

"Brigsby?" Her father chuckled over his bottle of beer. "You mean that old felt bear you had, Keith?"

"Yeah. Abby used to sleep with him in the summer when she got scared." Uncle Keith gave the scruff of Abby's neck a playful rub. "Probably too old for that now, but I thought you'd like to see him again."

"You were inseparable from that bear when we were kids," Abby's father said.

"Come on, in this house? I needed something when I had bad dreams."

"Christ, you wet the bed so much your mattress almost doubled as a raft."

"I was a kid." Uncle Keith chuckled along with Abby's father, but Abby could feel the tension coming from his body. "A bear was more helpful than my super brave older brother telling a five-year-old to man up and stop crying about imaginary things."

"They were imaginary, and Grandma giving you a bear to fight the monsters didn't do anything to help, no matter what she said."

"It helped me," Abby said.

Abby's father gave her a surprised glance, as did Uncle Keith. She wondered if she'd spoken out of turn, but a part of her felt it was worth it to stop the teasing that was slowly becoming a fight. Abby felt the tension creep around her stomach like a hungry snake.

"It gave me something to cuddle without going in to bother Uncle Keith and Aunt Sandra," Abby added.

Uncle Keith looked down, and the snake's coils around Abby's stomach turned to ice. "He's good for decoration," Abby added. "And memories."

"Well, not to break up the trip down memory lane," Abby's father said as he stood up. He took one last gulp of beer. "But Denise and I are probably gonna hit the road here in a little bit."

Abby and Uncle Keith both looked at her father in surprise. "You're leaving already?" Abby asked.

"We said we weren't going to stay the night, remember?"

"But I figured you'd stay for dinner," Uncle Keith said. "Maybe visit for a bit—"

"We'll plan to stay overnight when we come pick Abby up."

Uncle Keith nodded. Abby figured it'd be best to take a cue from him. He knew when there was no discussion to be had. She'd already ruined things by bringing up Brigsby. Abby wondered with a pang of guilt if talking about Brigsby had made her father decide to leave sooner. Between that and her mentioning Aunt Sandra, she made a silent vow to try and not let her big mouth ruin any more of her family's day.

"Looks like you'll have a peaceful week up here, Abby," her father said as everyone walked to the front door. "No one's at the beach today, at least."

Abby decided not to mention the woman in the baseball cap. Contradicting her father once was enough for that afternoon.

"Not too peaceful though," Uncle Keith said with a grin as he playfully punched Abby's upper arm. "I'm putting you to work first thing."

"Can we paint the bathroom first?"

Uncle Keith laughed—a hearty one, without any sadness at all. It cheered Abby up. "You bet. Get that hideous green out of there."

"Have fun, Abby," her mother said as she stooped down to give her a hug. Abby leaned in and her mother kissed her cheek. "Call us if you need anything," she whispered. Abby nodded against her shoulder.

"See you soon," her father said as he also gave Abby a quick hug. He stood up, then shook hands with Uncle Keith. "You too," her father said.

"Yup. Good to see you guys," Uncle Keith said.

Her parents turned and walked out the door. Abby and Uncle Keith stood in the hallway, still and silent even as they heard the car drive away.

Uncle Keith looked at Abby. He seemed less sure of himself. It struck Abby that they were alone, and would be alone for a whole week. They'd spent hours together alone, even a quick overnight alone; but never a whole week. Abby began to feel awkward, and in the moments of silence between them, she found herself wishing for Aunt Sandra or one of her parents to fill the void.

Uncle Keith smiled a little. "Well, I was originally going to make dinner for everyone, but if it's just the two of us, I'll order a pizza. How's that sound?"

"Sounds great!"

"I can order delivery, but the best is from a place that only does carry-out. You mind?"

"No, I can ride in the car again if it's a short trip." Abby's knees begged to differ, but she ignored them.

"Oh, I can go pick it up. You can get settled in."

"Oh." Abby was already settled in, but she got the sense that Uncle Keith wanted to go alone. Already.

"Or, I mean, you can come if you want. I just didn't think you'd want to be in the car again so soon, and it'll be less than 30 minutes—"

"It's okay. I'll wait here."

"Alright. Well, I'll head out in a few and have it ASAP." Uncle Keith stooped and held out his arms.

Abby looked at him curiously. "It's just 30 minutes," she said.

Uncle Keith chuckled a bit and straightened back up. "It's not that, it's—well, it's dawning on me how long it's been since I've seen you. Just felt like giving you another hug, I guess."

Abby softened a little.

"But you're too old for random uncle hugs, I get it." He laughed, but stopped when Abby moved forward and gave him a quick hug. He hugged her back and patted her shoulder.

"I'll be back soon," Uncle Keith said as he grabbed his jacket. "You still like pepperoni?"

"Yup," Abby said.

"Great." Uncle Keith left. Abby went into the kitchen and looked out the window. She focused on the waves moving back and forth over the sand. It helped her feel a little less lonely.

———

Uncle Keith returned and came into the kitchen with a box of pizza. "La comida es preparada," he said.

"It's 'la cena está servida,'" Abby corrected with a smile as they walked into the kitchen. Abby's stomach growled as Uncle Keith set the pizza on the table.

"Ah. My Spanish's been rusty since I stopped taking it in high school. Elena tells me to not even try."

"Who's Elena?"

"The calculus teacher at Sangway High. We'd get drinks after work sometimes."

"Do you still hang out even though—" Abby stopped herself from referencing Uncle Keith's job, not wanting a repeat of what happened earlier that afternoon.

"Even though I got fired?" He gave a sardonic grin, but Abby looked down all the same.

"It's okay, Skipper." Uncle Keith patted Abby's wrist, and she looked up to see him giving her a warm smile. "We all know I got fired and I got dumped. We're going to have a pretty quiet visit if we can't talk about any of those things while you're here."

"I just didn't want to make you uncomfortable like I did earlier."

"The hurt catches me offguard sometimes, yeah. I was with Sandra for ten years, and she's only been gone for a few weeks. It's going to sting sometimes to hear her name. But I'm also not going to pretend she doesn't exist or that she was never here. It's a sting I need to get used to." Unce Keith picked up a piece of pizza. "You'll understand when you have your heart broken for the first time. I never know with teens—are you dating now, or still too young for boys—or hey, girls, I don't know—"

"I'm not dating anyone. Everyone at my school is boring." There was one boy, Jake, in her English class that had nice eyes and a nicer voice; and Abby sometimes found her gaze lingering on Stacy's hair and clothes. But dating had yet to really cross her mind. Crushes always seemed like something she made herself think about when asked, as opposed to simply having them.

Uncle Keith laughed. "Well, maybe you'll have better luck in high school." He took a bite, then added, "But, yes, Elena and I still hang out. She refers to our old boss as Principal Pendejo in solidarity."

"Ooh, no es bueno," Abby teased.

"You know what that means?"

"Yeah. Carmen calls people that all the time."

"Well, as long as you don't call your principal that, I won't take responsibility for swearing in Spanish in front of you."

Abby chuckled as she thought of this woman trash-talking the principal of Sangway High, which kept her from feeling sad again about how Principal Moss thought she'd been scared of a stupid ghost story. "So, what're we going to work on first?" Abby asked. "In the house, I mean."

"Well, I figure we can dive into painting or something tomorrow," Uncle Keith said. "I've got an all-day shift the day after tomorrow, and—"

"Shift? You got another job already?"

"A summer one, at least; until I can find something a little more stable. You remember the wharf? I'm working at the bookstore there now."

"Oh. Cool." Abby looked outside and saw the waves crashing onto the shore with a little added fervor as the evening tide came in.

"You can come to the wharf with me on the days I have to work, though."

"Can I help with anything at the store?"

"Oh, you don't have to stay in the store for my whole shift. There're a lot of new shops there. I figure you can look around, and then we can catch up after I get off work."

"Oh." Abby frowned. She hadn't even been in Sangway Bluff for twelve hours, and already, Uncle Keith was pushing her away while he did his own thing.

"I work about eight hours on Tuesday," Uncle Keith continued. "So I can drive you home after lunch if you get bored."

Now she wasn't even welcome at the wharf—Uncle Keith wanted her home, home alone, halfway through his shift. He'd probably ask her to fix the house for him too. She took a bite of pizza and didn't respond.

"I know it's not as fun as when I had the whole summer off," Uncle Keith said. "But—"

"But it's different now, I know," Abby said. "Since you got fired."

She regretted it as soon as it left her mouth. She put down her pizza and looked up at Uncle Keith, who glared at her. "I'm sorry," Abby said.

"Don't worry about it," Uncle Keith said as he picked up his pizza. "I said you could talk about it."

"I'm just sad we can't spend more time together. I'm sad that—"

"Everything's different? Yeah, me too." Abby was about to clarify, but Uncle Keith continued, "In fact, no one's more upset about it than me. Maybe try and remember that before you bite my head off. I'm trying, Abby, I really am."

"I know. I'm sorry."

Uncle Keith nodded, but Abby saw his glare soften. She swallowed, then said, "Can I ask one thing about that, though?"

"Sure." Uncle Keith gave a half smile. "Just nicely."

"Why were you fired?"

Uncle Keith chewed his last bite a little more slowly. He set the crust down, then sighed. Abby stayed quiet and also stayed still, to show him she wouldn't move on from the question.

"It can get tough teaching kids year in and year out," he said. "Especially when they disappear or you see bad things happen to them and know there's nothing you can do except be there to listen. Around here, there aren't a lot of resources for kids who aren't from blue blood families. I saw a lot of brilliant kids slip through the cracks, smart kids who didn't put their best foot forward because they knew college wasn't an option. It wears you out, even when you enjoy teaching.

"But I had a student this past year, Claire"—Uncle Keith swallowed—"who was great. She got accepted at Brown. I knew she was going to make it. And then she—she didn't."

"Why? Did she flunk out?"

Uncle Keith swallowed again. "She died. Well, disappeared. The police are looking, but no one's really confident about finding her. You don't just get lost around here, you know?"

"And you don't think she ran away?"

"No." Uncle Keith took a sip of water. "I mean, she may have. But it's not the first time kids have disappeared in Sangway Bluff. Back when your dad and I were kids, there was a summer camp—a sleepaway camp out on Blueberry Island—"

"The one out that way?" Abby jerked her thumb towards the kitchen window, which had a view of three small islands far off the coast. Uncle Keith used to take her by the islands when they'd go boating, though they'd never visited any of them. She'd figured they were off-limits to people.

"Yeah. But the camp got shut down because one summer, four kids and a counselor were killed."

"Jesus! Like Camp Crystal Lake?" Abby went cold at her outburst, but Uncle Keith laughed a little.

"Not quite like that, no," he said. "But it was bad—bad enough to shut down the camp and bad enough to traumatize the town. It was the first big murder like that, you know, one that makes the papers and gets people talking. CNN was here for months."

"What does that have to do with Claire?"

"Another kid disappears, and even when it's twenty years later, those same tongues start wagging. You get the true crime people, the news, the gossipers and superstitious. And then you get people like me—people who live here and just want to mourn their dead. People who are just tired. I got tired, Skipper. I got tired of everything, so tired that Principal Pendejo didn't think I had it in me for another year."

Abby couldn't quite believe that tiredness was enough to get someone fired, but she could tell from Uncle Keith's weary expression that that was all he wanted to say about it. "Well, I'm sorry you lost your job," Abby said. "And I'm sorry about Claire."

"Thanks."

"And Aunt Sandra, and all the gossip, and—"

"I've got it, thanks." Uncle Keith gave a faint nod and a smile to match. "Let's not talk about that. Let's talk about what color to paint the bathroom. First task, right?"

Abby smiled. "Right."

CHAPTER 6

Abby woke up the next morning feeling refreshed. The sound of the waves was soothing, and a soft bed had eased the ache of a long drive. As she walked down the hall, she looked at the walls and doors with fresh eyes, wondering what she and Uncle Keith would work on first.

She walked into the kitchen and saw Uncle Keith moving hurriedly through his morning prep, from sipping coffee to running his free fingers through his hair. "Morning," Abby said.

Uncle Keith jumped a little, then looked apologetic. "I'm glad you're up," he said. "I—"

"You in a hurry to get started?" Abby asked as she grabbed a box of cereal from the counter. "You could've woken me up if you wanted to get to work on the house."

"That's the thing: I can't today. Not this morning, anyway."

Abby paused as she opened the box. "What do you mean? Why not?"

Uncle Keith sighed as he set down his mug. "I was supposed to have today off, but Marion called in sick; and Chloe can't run the store herself, so—"

Abby had no clue who these women were, and didn't get why Uncle Keith expected her to know. Telling her, though, would mean talking to her; something he was obviously in a hurry to stop doing.

"So I have to open up the bookstore," Uncle Keith said. "I'm really sorry, I know it's your first day here."

"It's fine," Abby said to her empty cereal bowl.

"No, it isn't. I'm honestly pretty pissed right now."

Abby looked up, and saw that Uncle Keith's expression matched his words. "I told them about you and about working on the house, but—"

Abby softened. "Marion's sick. She can't help it."

"No, but Steve can; and he passed on helping today." Keith rolled his eyes as he took a last swig of his coffee. "I can't believe he's been there so long, he almost never works."

"Who's Steve?"

"A jackass." Uncle Keith grabbed his keys and stopped by Abby's side. "I should be home by lunch," he said. "You'll be okay here by yourself, right?"

"Yeah, I can stay home alone."

"Great." Uncle Keith leaned down and gave Abby a quick hug. "Call me if you need anything."

"Do you want me to do any work on the house?" Abby called as he exited the kitchen, even though Abby wasn't sure what she could do on her own.

"Sure! Do what you want."

"What do you want—"

The door slammed shut, and Abby turned to the table. She shoved the empty bowl away, no longer hungry.

Even if Abby had known what work she could do on the house without Uncle Keith, she had no desire to do it. She spent her first hour alone sulking on a faded couch in the living room, its beige and dirtied white stripes a perfect setting for her sour mood. When she grew bored pouting at the water-stained ceiling, she'd play Candy Crush, her thumbs like saws slicing through the colorful lines of candy.

After a while, she grew bored with both the game and her bad mood. Uncle Keith had to work. There wasn't anything either of them could do about it. He'd also be home after lunch, and though she was still upset that he'd been in such a hurry to get away from her—to go to work, he was just going to work—she wanted to at least try to be more cheerful by the time he came home.

She'd explored upstairs the day before, but she'd only spent time in the kitchen and on the old musty couch on the first floor. Abby walked from room to room. Most were empty except for the living room. There was a dining room with an empty table and no chairs, and a bathroom down the hallway, which stood next to a closed white door.

Abby stopped in front of the door. The scratches in the paint, which had been dark brown a moment ago, began to seep out blood like crimson tears.

For the first time since she'd started seeing trickles of blood in random places, Abby didn't feel afraid. She opened the door and walked down the steps. She took them one at a time, but only because it was dark. She could see the dead.

She had no reason to be afraid of them—especially when all they seemed to do when they saw her was get the hell away from her. *Can't run away in a musty old basement, though*, she thought with a smirk as she stopped at the final step.

She flicked on the light and was greeted by four pairs of bright yellow eyes looking out from bloodied faces.

Abby shrieked and flicked the light back off. She heard hissing as she scrambled for the light switch again. She turned it on, and a lone light bulb shone a single beam across an unfinished basement filled with boxes, a cement floor, and the ghosts of four dead children. They scurried away from the her like roaches from a kitchen light.

"Who are you?" Abby asked. She figured it was fruitless, and sure enough, the children turned their backs to her. They pounded the walls and slashed their palms across their throats, resembling rabid hamsters trying to clean their faces.

Abby ignored their snarls and stamped across the floor. "You can leave this fucking basement, you know. You're dead—can't you appear and disappear from places?"

They all growled, but the tallest one, a girl with shoulder-length, bloodied hair and a sundress, howled above the noise of the others. Abby moved towards her, and though the girl stayed facing the wall, she rushed away and scurried towards the wall of boxes. She switched between swiping her throat and smashing her fists against the boxes. It seemed like a manic ritual of fear, one that culminated in the cardboard growing dark with blood that began to weep over the girl's hair.

Abby's anger began to dissolve into fear. The growling of the other children sounded behind her like the waves she'd fallen asleep to the night before. The girl crumpled against the boxes, her fists pounding but with less vigor.

"Please," Abby said as quietly as she could. "Please tell me why."

The girl stopped pounding the boxes. She stood up, the blood from the boxes pooling at her feet. She spun around, her yellow eyes aflame with hatred that made Abby miss the bloody, gaping holes of the girl in Locker 751.

Instead of her eyes, though, it was the girl's throat that bled. A smooth, even slit stretched across her throat. Drops of blood came from cracks in the scar, which increased into rivers that stained the girl's dress and legs.

She stared at Abby with more hate than she'd ever seen in her life. She opened her mouth and let out a scream that sounded like the harshest, fastest wind of a hurricane.

Three more screams sounded behind her, all gusts of wind like the girl's. Abby spun around and saw the three other children—three boys, she now saw—with the same bleeding slits across their throats. They screamed with a ferocity that was only surpassed by the hate in their eyes.

Abby ran towards the stairs and turned off the light. She heard their roars and rasps until she slammed the door shut behind her. Even with the newfound silence, she didn't want to stay anywhere near the basement. She ran outside, ran onto the beach, planning to run until she found a parking lot or a rock cliff or somewhere quiet to collect her bearings.

She skidded to a stop when she saw a woman walking along the shore. Abby had a sinking feeling that she was the only one who could see her.

The woman kept walking in her direction. She wore a baseball cap, t-shirt, and long white skirt. Her clothes and her skin were free of blood. She saw Abby looking at her and stopped, then hurried towards her. Abby grew hopeful—maybe she wasn't dead. Or maybe she was, and she would actually speak to her.

As the woman neared, Abby saw curls of skin rise up from her body like smoke. The curls left her body transparent. Blood began to fill the spaces they left behind, swirling and pooling as her skin flayed itself in front of her.

Abby screamed and spun around before the woman could approach her. She ran towards the house and hoped that the woman wouldn't follow her.

"Abby?"

Abby looked up from her bed. Uncle Keith had called from downstairs, but she didn't feel like getting up. It was bright outside, but almost dinnertime. Uncle Keith had texted saying he couldn't leave after lunch—*Steve says he's sick, bet you anything he's partying on the coast somewhere*, he'd written—but Abby had only replied with, *K*. She was too exhausted from the events of the morning to care whether or not her uncle was home.

Abby ate some cheese and crackers for lunch, then spent the rest of the day upstairs in her room. She was too frightened to explore the rest of the house. Seeing things was one thing, but bleeding boxes and roaring children were too much for her nerves.

She sat with a book she'd last read when she was eight years old and up for her summer visit. Brigsby sat beside her on the bed, close enough so that his felt fur touched her leg. Her father would think she was regressing, just like he'd feared when the teddy bear first came up. Abby didn't care. Her father wasn't there. Brigsby was, and Brigsby wouldn't tell her that everything she'd seen had just been her fears.

"There you are." Uncle Keith leaned against her doorway.

"Hey Uncle Keith," Abby said, sitting up and setting her book on the bedside table. "How was work?"

"Busy. Good for the shop, bad for me." He sighed, then said, "Look, I'm really sorry I couldn't be here today. I wanted to—"

"I know. It's okay."

"I know this visit is important for you—"

"I don't care! Really!"

Uncle Keith looked wounded. "Really, I don't mind," Abby said. "Please stop apologizing to me."

Uncle Keith chuckled a little. "Sandra used to tell me that too." He straightened, the sorrow gone from his face. "Well, my normal shift is tomorrow."

Abby tried to keep her shoulders up, and tried not to show her fear at being alone in the house for another day.

"But I'm thinking you can come with me. Want to see the store?"

"Yeah!" Abby tempered her eagerness. "Yeah, I think that'd be good," she said.

"Great. So, what'd you do today? Explore around the house?"

Abby hesitated for a moment. Part of her wondered what Uncle Keith would say if she told him about the children in the basement and the woman on the beach.

"A little bit," Abby said. "It's so old. Carmen would love it—she loves ghosts and stuff, and this place looks super haunted."

Uncle Keith smiled, but uncomfortably. "Don't let your dad hear you say that. The last thing he or our parents ever wanted to hear was a ghost story, especially about their own house."

Abby thought of how her father reacted when she brought up scary things she'd seen. He'd looked at her with concern, fear, worry, and judgment. She didn't want to see any of those things on Uncle Keith's face.

"Well, today was fine," Abby said. "I mostly just sat up here and read."

CHAPTER 7

The drive to the wharf was much shorter now that Abby and her uncle were staying by the shore. Abby remembered the excitement she'd had at the prospect of a long drive to the coast, one that usually led to a long boat ride on the water. Today, though, they'd be on land and around the shops that called the wharf home.

"I don't remember a bookstore on the wharf," Abby said as Uncle Keith parked. "Is it new?"

"It's one of the only shops that isn't new," Uncle Keith replied. "We just didn't bring you in a lot because they didn't have a good selection of kids books." He grinned at her as they walked towards the dock. "But now you're thirteen and can read whatever you want, right?"

"Nothing too adult," Abby said. "Mom says nothing with shirtless men on the cover or—"

"Okay, okay, I was just kidding." Uncle Keith shoved his hands in his pockets and fixed his gaze ahead, though with embarrassment or irritation, Abby wasn't sure. She felt bad either way.

"Well, we've got a bigger kids' section now," Uncle Keith continued. "And young adult, new adult, and regular, boring adult for all your reading needs." They walked by a line of stores that Abby didn't remember at all from her previous visits. There'd mostly been food shacks and a couple souvenir shops. Now the dock was lined with boutiques and a gourmet grocery store. Abby doubted she'd be able to get the lobster roll she'd dreamed of on the way to Sangway Bluff—not unless she wanted to buy premium lobster from the gourmet shop.

They stopped in front of the last building before the wharf opened entirely to the dock, which held nothing but a view of the water. Abby looked at the faded teal paint on the walls of the store and vaguely remembered running by it on her way to the edge of the dock with a handful of sunflower seeds to feed the seagulls.

Uncle Keith unlocked the shop and turned on the lights. Abby looked around. It wasn't as big as the bookstore in the mall that she went to at home, and it had the same smell as her local library: old, faded paper that seemed prevalent even with all of the new titles facing forward on a display shelf.

"Not bad, huh?" Uncle Keith said as he shut the door behind them. He walked next to Abby and looked around the store with her, as if he didn't see it every time he came into work. "Betsy—she's the owner—she did me a solid, hiring me on short notice. Guess buying books for my students from here all the time got me some clout."

"So what do you do now?"

"Well, I'm working the register until Chloe gets here. And then I'll be doing inventory, then bringing new books out here—you know, fun stuff."

"Sounds like it," Abby said with a smile.

"The other stores'll be opening up soon, so you'll be able to poke around in them until my lunch break."

Abby tried not to scrunch her face at the thought of poking around in a neon Lilly Pulitzer shop. "I want to hang out in here though," she said. "I don't mind. Can I help with anything?"

"I don't think so. A lot of this stuff needs training—"

"Even putting books on the shelves? I know how to alphabetize."

"There're categories and stuff too, Skipper."

Abby pouted a little before she could stop herself. Uncle Keith sighed, but his expression was kind. "Look," he added. "I appreciate you wanting to help, but you'll be helping plenty at the house; and even though I'm the only one here now, we've got plenty of employees here to do bookstore work."

It wasn't about helping, though—it was about spending time with Uncle Keith. But Abby kept that to herself. She didn't want to sound like a baby. He was also right: there was the house, which they would work on together.

"Hey Keith!" A young woman with lime green hair and a septum piercing walked through the door. "You can't keep getting here so early—you're making me look bad."

"Get here earlier and you'll look better," he said with a grin.

The woman took out her AirPods and widened her grin to unimaginable proportions when she saw Abby. "Is this your niece?" she said, her voice reaching octaves that were dangerously close to summoning every dog in Sangway Bluff. "Hi! I'm Chloe."

"Abby," Abby said, her stomach curling into itself.

"Wow, you're so tall!"

"You've never seen me before."

Chloe laughed uncomfortably and Uncle Keith gave Abby a quick, sharp look. "Be nice," he said. Abby frowned at being reprimanded by her uncle in front of a stranger.

"Oh, she's just getting to know me," Chloe said with a wave of her hand. "I just figured you'd be—well, I don't see teenagers a lot, what do I know about height? Not as much as you, Keith, with your old job."

Uncle Keith flinched a little, but still replied, "I taught seniors, not middle schoolers."

"Well, I better get to the register before I embarrass myself in front of Abby any more than I already have!" Chloe laughed again, and Abby began to consider how badly she wanted to stay in the bookstore. "Let me know if you want any YA recommendations, sweetie—I've read some good ones this past year."

"I will," Abby said with absolutely no intention to do so.

"And I'm gonna tackle the storeroom," Uncle Keith said with a nod. Chloe walked towards the register, and Uncle Keith nodded towards a shelf on the other side of the store. "You should check out some of the books back there," he said. "Lots to look at."

Abby realized Uncle Keith was directing her away from Chloe, and she gave a small smile in thanks. He nodded and gave a small wink before disappearing into the back room.

Abby slid her fingertips along the spines of all the books. Most were the same books she'd seen everywhere before, but she wasn't desperate enough for new material to check out the Staff Recommendations shelf that was right next to the cash register—though part of her wondered what Chloe found interesting to read, so she could avoid it.

She stopped at a table with a small display. A yellow sign declared in simple typed letters: *LOCAL LORE: Books About Sangway Bluff and the Surrounding Islands*. Abby picked up a book with a black-and-white photograph of the beach on its cover. She flipped through and saw nothing of interest—mostly colonial history and tourist destinations she'd already visited.

A black book with gold letters eerily promised the best ghost stories on the island. Abby reached towards it with interest, then moved her hand away. She'd had enough actual ghosts yesterday to last the whole week.

Her eyes wandered towards a newer-looking book, with a glossy cover and a stark photograph of one of the islands near Uncle Keith's house. It was called *Blueberry Hell: The Untold Story of the Sangway Summer Camp Murders*. Abby's eyes widened. She remembered Uncle Keith's story from her first night there. He hadn't wanted to talk about the summer camp murders on Blueberry Island—but the book would.

Abby flipped to the opening chapter and began to read.

Blueberry Island is one of three islands off the coast of Sangway Bluff. Its lush forests, extensive hiking paths, and wild blueberry bushes made it a popular spot for an annual summer camp. Kids aged ten to thirteen would camp for three weeks and brush up on their survival skills.

Those skills, though, were no match against something that nature couldn't predict: murder.

In August 1989, four campers and their counselor went into the forest to tell ghost stories, a tradition they'd started amongst themselves.

It seemed, though, that a ghost story was the least of their fears.

"Whatcha reading, Skipper?"

Abby looked up and saw Uncle Keith smiling at her. The smile disappeared when she flipped the book over to show him. "These are the camp murders you told me about, right?" she asked.

"Yeah, but I don't want you reading this," Uncle Keith said as he plucked the book from her hands.

"Why not? I can handle gross stuff."

"It's not that it's gross. It's exploitative."

"How?"

"It treats the murders like an episode of some crime show. It tells it like a horror story, or like something those true crime fans can lap up and blog about. But it's not a game. Kids died. Their families still live here."

"Then why do you have it in the store?"

"Wasn't my call to make." Uncle Keith returned it to the table, but placed it behind the book of ghost stories.

"Well, what would you say about the murders?" Abby asked.

Uncle Keith looked at her with a furrowed brow. "What do you mean?"

"You don't like what the book has to say. What would you say?"

"Why do you want to know? It's grisly, violent—"

"I don't care."

"And history. We don't need to keep drudging this up. Let the dead rest."

Abby frowned, and Uncle Keith pointed at the book. "You're also better than books like this. Find something less sensational and more informative to read."

Abby kept her frown, but she couldn't help but feel a little proud that Uncle Keith thought she was too smart for those types of stories. Still, she wanted to know more. Once Uncle Keith moved towards another aisle, she slipped the book under her arm and moved towards the graphic novels. Abby sat on the floor and continued to read:

While the details are sketchy—everyone that had been at the scene of the crime, after all, was dead—police deduced that the killings were a murder-suicide. It's believed that Mary Pelham, a seventeen-year-old camp counselor, murdered the four campers—Michael Nills (eleven), Joel Rowan (eleven), Jonah Reece (eleven), and Felicity Knight (twelve)—before taking her own life.

"It was horrific to see," recounts Kevin Willard, a fellow counselor who found the scene of the crime the next morning. "The kids had slit necks and were splayed on the dirt in an even circle, like quarters of a clock; and Mary swung from a tree branch between them. It almost looked like it was set up by someone else."

Perhaps it was. Some have speculated that the murder-suicide was just a murder.

Abby stopped reading. Four kids and one woman—well, one teenager, but still, older than the others. The mention of slit necks brought an image that was all too clear in her mind. Abby slid her thumb across the bottom of the book's pages. Halfway through, she felt the standard paper turn to gloss: photographs. She took a breath, then flipped the book open to the photos.

Even though she had a good idea of what she was about to see, she still jumped at the sight of the four children's final school photos. Their hair, skin, and eyes were colorful and happy. They were alive.

And Abby had seen them, dead and angry, in her uncle's basement.

CHAPTER 8

There was no way Uncle Keith could be responsible.

Abby closed the book and set it aside. The children had to be in his basement for another reason. Maybe they'd floated over from Blueberry Island and stopped at the first house they found. Maybe the counselor had brought them there. But then why would she be on the beach and not in the house? And why did Uncle Keith not want to talk about it at all if he had nothing about it to hide?

Abby shook her head. It was ridiculous to think he was involved.

She glanced at the book, and in a sudden, refreshing moment of recall, she remembered the year the murders took place: 1989.

Abby pulled out her iPhone and did some quick math. Uncle Keith was thirty-eight. He would've been eight years old when the murders happened. He hadn't been old enough to hang a seventeen-year-old girl from a tree. He hadn't even been old enough to attend the camp.

So why did the story bother him so much—and why were the victims in his basement?

"Oh! Jesus, you scared me!"

Abby looked up and saw Chloe laughing, a stack of books gone askew in her hands.

"Almost tripped over you," Chloe said as she straightened the books. "It wouldn't go over well with your uncle if I stepped on you during my shift."

"Sorry," Abby said, standing. Chloe shrugged and kept her grin as she placed a graphic novel on the shelf. Abby wondered if she had any emotions that weren't pure exuberance.

"No worries! I got used to dodging kids in the aisles. Keith's students came here to buy books he suggested in class." Chloe sighed, but even that sounded somewhat cheerful—more whimsical than sad, like when one remembered a place they visited one summer and never returned to. "It's too bad he won't be teaching there anymore. He was like a walking staff recommendation even before he worked here."

"Pretty bad for him too," Abby added pointedly.

"Oh yeah, of course. I just saw his students almost all the time. Claire used to come in here almost every day with the latest recommendation from Mr. Gillman—" Chloe stopped herself, pursed her lips in an embarrassed smile, and said, "Well, I'll let you get back to reading."

Even if Abby hadn't been frightened by what she'd been reading, she would've lost all interest in it with the mention of Claire. "You mean the same Claire who died?" Abby asked as she followed Chloe down the aisle. Chloe halted, and Abby added, "Or disappeared?"

"You're pretty blunt, aren't you?" Chloe asked as she turned around. Abby saw a pointed frown on Chloe's face, and felt a surprising rush of guilt at the sight of it.

"She disappeared, and she's probably dead," Chloe continued. "I know you're visiting and probably just curious, but it's still fresh for a lot of us here, especially those of us who knew her."

Abby remembered Uncle Keith's pained expression when he mentioned her, and felt even worse. "I'm sorry," Abby said sincerely. "I should've known better. Uncle Keith was still upset about the Blueberry Island murders, and those were 30 years ago. I can only imagine what everyone here is feeling about something that happened recently."

"Yeah. Your uncle gets mad about Blueberry Island, but Claire—" Chloe looked around, likely looking for Uncle Keith. She stooped a little lower and dropped her voice. "He was devastated about Claire. I know they were close—in a totally cool way, no student-teacher thing—"

Chloe laughed awkwardly, and Abby tried to keep gross thoughts of Uncle Keith in a student-teacher fling out of her head.

"But when she disappeared, it hit him hard."

"Hard enough to lose his job, right?"

Chloe nodded. "The disappearance and the hubbub surrounding it would be hard on anyone."

"What hubbub? The news and stuff?"

"Yeah. Coverage." Chloe's eyes flitted in a way that made Abby think she wasn't sharing everything. Before she could press, Chloe added, "I just wanted to let you know so you wouldn't ask him too much about things that might upset him. I heard you guys arguing about the Blueberry Island murders—"

"We weren't arguing," Abby said as an embarrassed flush swam up her throat to her cheeks. How dare Chloe listen in on them?

"And I'm not going to tell you what to talk about with your own uncle—"

"Of course you won't. You're not my mom. You're not even an adult. You look like a little kid on Halloween with that stupid hair."

Chloe glared down at her. Abby snapped her mouth shut.

"I am an adult," Chloe said in an even, deep voice. "And even at my most immature, I act less childish than you're acting right now."

Abby looked down. She was in no mood to argue or apologize—certainly not to Chloe.

"Just be more sensitive when talking about scary things, alright?" Chloe turned away before Abby could answer, ending their conversation. Abby snorted quietly to herself. *Sensitivity to scary things, my ass.* Chloe had no idea what it meant to be scared. She hadn't seen four dead kids in the basement and their counselor on the beach.

But Abby couldn't tell her that without sounding crazy or, worse, like a scared little girl. She sighed and looked at the clock. It was going to be another long day alone with her thoughts.

———

After walking up and down the aisles once more, Abby decided to take Uncle Keith's suggestion to explore the wharf. "I'm going for a walk," Abby called as she approached the door. "In case Uncle Keith asks." She exited before Chloe could answer.

Abby walked towards the water. She had no interest in visiting the shops, but the sun was shining over the water, creating a beautiful view of the islands. Abby smiled as she took in the green trees and rocky shores of each island. Blueberry Island stood between Holly Oak Island and Crane's Despot. She'd visited none of them, but Aunt Sandra had once told her that Crane's Despot was haunted by the ghost of a Viking king. If Uncle Keith would take her out there, maybe Abby could confirm whether or not the story was true.

Abby sat on a bench, so absorbed in the islands that she almost didn't notice the two boys sitting on the bench beside hers. It was only when one of them laughed that she became aware of their presence. She glanced in their direction. They were older boys, probably high schoolers. They were talking and didn't notice Abby. Abby returned her attention to the ocean.

"You hear Mr. Gillman's working in that bookshop now?"

Abby's attention perked up. She kept her gaze on the islands, but did her best to listen.

"Yeah." The boy who answered didn't sound pleased.

"Guess you won't be going in there, huh?"

"Not unless I can ask him questions the police obviously won't."

"You still think he's responsible?"

"I know he had something to do with Claire."

Abby's eyebrows shot up. The other boy chuckled. "Yeah, but you thought they were doing stuff before she disappeared."

"I didn't think they were doing stuff. I know Claire wasn't interested. But Mr. Gillman was totally being a creep. Giving her 'special' books to read, helping her look for colleges outside of Massachusetts, saying she could do better. And those meetings after school?"

"You mean the enriched reading program?"

"Enriched reading, my ass. Even when they were meeting at the school, Mr. Gillman always looked irritated when I'd come by to pick her up, like I was interrupting something. And when they started meeting at the diner? He was totally trying to take her on dates."

Abby's neck grew hot, and she bit her lip to keep from interrupting them and defending Uncle Keith. He wouldn't act that way around one of his students. She'd believed that even before Chloe had defended Keith and Claire's friendship earlier.

"Come on, Max," his friend said. "They started doing that when her debate club schedule changed."

"You're telling me they can't meet any other day after school—and at the school? You on his side, man?"

"Hey, I don't know what happened. None of us do. It was definitely weird, though."

"Weird, and suspicious."

"I also thought it was weird he just went home after the cops talked to him, no booking or nothing."

Abby's skin went cold. The cops had spoken to Uncle Keith?

"You know my grandpa used to work with Sheriff Gillman?" Max's friend continued. "Mr. Gillman's dad? I wouldn't be surprised if the cops let him off easy because his dad was a cop. Looking out for their own, you know?"

"Well, they better look out for Claire," Max huffed. "Otherwise, I'm gonna start looking."

"Let's start by looking for some food."

The two boys got up and wandered away. Abby stayed seated, staring straight out at the ocean but no longer looking at the islands. Why had the cops spoken to Uncle Keith? And why was Max convinced that Uncle Keith was involved with Claire's disappearance? It seemed his only involvement was concern over her whereabouts, something any teacher close with his students would worry about.

Either way, Abby felt worse than she had in the bookshop, even after her argument with Chloe. It seemed the more she heard about what was going on in Sangway Bluff, the less she liked.

CHAPTER 9

Abby returned to the bookshop and saw Uncle Keith at the cash register talking to Chloe. Abby wondered if Chloe had told him what happened between them. He was smiling as he spoke, though; so if he'd heard, he wasn't too upset.

"Hey Skipper," he said. "How was your walk?"

"Okay. Can I go back to the house after lunch?"

"Bored already?"

"I just figured I can actually do some work on it," Abby lied.

"Chloe, I'll be back in thirty," Uncle Keith said as he walked towards Abby.

"Okay!" She smiled and waved at Abby, which threw her. "Nice to meet you."

Abby wondered if Chloe was pretending to be nice, or if she was genuinely over their fight. Either way, Abby didn't want to spend the rest of the day wandering around the bookstore and avoiding Chloe's company. She answered, "You too," and exited with Uncle Keith.

After Uncle Keith dropped her off—with a promise to be home for dinner and to bring home something special—Abby thought of the vast loneliness of her grandparents' house. She wondered what it'd been like for Uncle Keith and her father to live here as kids. Had they found the long halls and large rooms fun to play in, or caverns that could swallow them whole?

"Abby!"

Abby grinned the moment she saw Carmen's face appear on her phone. She hadn't realized how much she missed her. "Hey, what's up?" Abby said as she reclined on the couch.

"Oh, you know, the usual: bored as shit in Phillip's Glen." Carmen rolled her eyes and blew a stray chunk of hair out of her face. "What are you calling me for? Aren't you supposed to be doing Habitat for Humanity or something on your uncle's house?"

"Yeah, but nothing's happening because he's had to work."

"He's not off work for your visit?"

"No." Abby felt her annoyance with Uncle Keith began to simmer. She did her best to temper it.

"Well hey, free rein in the house! Show me around, let me see it!"

"Come on, I just sat down!"

"From doing what? Sitting all day? You're on vacation! Let me see it, you cow!"

"Fine, fine!" Abby laughed as she stood up. She took Carmen on a tour of the upstairs and downstairs, making a point not to linger too long near the basement door. Carmen ooh'd and ah'd throughout like a prospective buyer checking out a new house.

"Man, I bet that house is haunted as shit." Carmen laughed, and Abby hoped she couldn't see her face grow pale. "Any ghost stories about it?"

"Not the house, but there are some about the town itself and the surrounding islands."

"I bet. An old Massachusetts coast town? This whole damn state's haunted." The view of Carmen's face bent at an angle that suggested she'd set her phone up via PopSocket. Sure enough, Abby heard the distinct clicking of Carmen plugging away on her parents' laptop.

"There was also a murder-suicide here in the nineties."

"Ooh!" Carmen typed faster.

"You sounded like such a psychopath just now. 'Ooh, let me look up the murder!'"

"I'm just reading stories! Real psychopaths wouldn't be excited by this stuff; they'd just be studying it."

"What do you know about psychopaths?"

"Plenty—and it looks like there's plenty of murders out there too."

"There aren't, like, tons or anything. There were five victims in the summer camp one—"

"No, not that one. Some high school girl disappeared this year! Claire Baxter. Watch out Abby, there's someone on the prowl!"

Abby didn't reply, but rather went cold. Carmen looked at the phone and knit her brow in concern. "Too far?" she asked. "They don't really know if Claire's dead, she's just—"

"Gone, I know. Sorry. I heard about her before and you caught me off-guard."

"Sorry."

Carmen went back to scrolling and reading. After a few moments, Abby smiled. "Are you gonna look up psychopath stories, or are you going to talk to me?"

Carmen didn't reply. She paused from typing and pursed her lips.

"Carmen? What's up?"

"Oh. Uh, noth—"

"Don't you dare say nothing. I can see you."

"Fine." She sighed, then said, "Your uncle's name is Keith, right?"

Abby's stomach turned to ice. "Yeah. Why?"

"Um, you're not gonna like this."

"What's up, ladies!" Carmen's brother Hector burst into view. He wagged his face in front of the camera and stuck out his tongue. "What're y'all doing, reading *Riverdale* slash fic out loud to each other?"

"Fuck off, Hector!" Carmen yelled. Abby felt like doing the same.

"It's my turn to use the computer. Gotta log my hours at the clam shack."

"Yeah, that's code for porn if I ever heard it."

"I'm not using our parents' computer for that! Come on, let me log on!"

"Carmen, what did you see about Uncle Keith?" Abby shouted, so Carmen would hear her over Hector being a dick.

"Right, hang on. Hector, MOVE!" Carmen turned back to the laptop while Hector stood to the side, tapping his foot while touching an imaginary watch on his wrist. Abby wanted to throttle him.

"Okay, I just emailed you the link," Carmen said, just as Abby's phone dinged with a new message. "I'll talk to you later, when Hector's being less of an asswipe."

"Keep calling me names and I won't drive you to the mall on the way to work anymore," Hector said.

"Yeah, run that by Mom, see what she says!" Carmen shot back.

"Bye Carmen!" Abby said, hoping she'd be heard, before hanging up.

She lay back on the bed and opened her email. Abby wondered how bad it could be. Was it worse than what she'd heard the two boys talking about at the wharf? Surely if it were that bad, Uncle Keith would be in jail or something. Certainly not working at the bookstore almost every day and talking about working on the house—talk that never seemed to culminate into actual work.

Abby shook her head. She was starting to sound like her father.

Maybe it was because the past couple days hadn't done much to prove her father wrong. Did she want to read something that would only worsen that feeling?

Ultimately, though, she was curious. She steeled herself and opened the article.

———

ENGLISH TEACHER QUESTIONED IN DISAPPEARANCE OF SANGWAY HIGH SENIOR

Claire Baxter last seen with Keith Gillman, who claims no involvement in her disappearance.

SANGWAY BLUFF, Mass.—*A Sangway Bluff High School teacher has been questioned in connection to the May 30 disappearance of 18-year-old Claire Baxter, authorities said.*

Keith Gillman, an English teacher, is believed to be the last person who saw Baxter at the Short Stack Diner on Seagull Avenue, a source with knowledge of the investigation said.

The source spoke under the condition of anonymity as they do not have authority to speak to the media.

It was previously reported that Baxter's boyfriend, Max Woods, 18, was the last person to see her at his home following a swim meet.

However, sources said Baxter's debit card was last used at the diner at 7:47 p.m. the night she disappeared.

"We knew Claire regularly met with Mr. Gillman at Short Stack," Cynthia Baxter, one of Claire's mothers, said. "He asked us if they could move their afterschool meetings there when her schedule changed. We were fine with it."

She said her wife, Maureen Mason-Baxter, knows Gillman socially through his girlfriend, Sandra Beacham. "We didn't realize Claire also saw Keith the night she disappeared. When she called us after seeing Max, she'd only said she was going for a drive."

Millicent Clark, owner of the Short Stack, recalled seeing Baxter and Gillman dining together that night and previous nights. Clark said Baxter and Gillman had been meeting at the diner "once a month or thereabouts" since January.

"They were going over school stuff, usually—papers, books, a couple college brochures." Clark said when she brought food or water to the table, "I wasn't listening to them, but when I'd lean in...they'd always be talking about Faulkner or Shelley or some other author."

Asked about their presence in the diner on the evening of Baxter's disappearance, Clark said, "I didn't think anything of it when I saw her here, and truthfully, I almost forgot until the police came by and said the diner was the last place she'd been."

Baxter has been the subject of a statewide search since her disappearance on May 30. The Massachusetts State Police and Sangway Bluff police have asked neighboring counties to report any sign of her, and will expand the investigation to neighboring states.

Police interviewed Gillman, a Sangway Bluff native and a teacher for fifteen years at Sangway Bluff High School, on June 10, after identifying him as the last person to see Baxter before she went missing.

State police investigators would not comment on the case, but the source with knowledge of the investigation said Gillman regularly met one-on-one with Baxter and other students as part of an enriched reading program. "He said they were going over the last book she'd read...and also talking about college," the source said. Baxter had recently been admitted to Brown University in Rhode Island. "He was giving her some advice."

Clark verified that Baxter left the diner before Gillman that evening. Gillman told police he then went to Blueberry Island for a late-night walk after leaving the diner alone.

Lucas Hodges, who watches the docks where Gillman keeps his boat, confirmed this.

"Unless Claire swam out there, she wasn't with Keith and he wasn't with her," Hodges told the Sangway Tribune. *He said hour-long nighttime walks on Blueberry Island are a customary pastime of Gillman's, but declined to comment further. The source said Gillman's alibi checked out and Beacham confirmed he had returned home by 10 p.m.*

Clark said there was one difference with Baxter and Gillman's last visit to the diner.

"The only thing I noticed was that they didn't have any school books this time. No papers, no brochures, nothing. It was like they were just there." Clark also recalled that as she approached the table to refill Baxter's soda, "Well, she snapped her mouth shut when I showed up, but before she saw me, I heard her say something about having to leave, and Keith looked upset."

Woods, a Sangway High School senior and Baxter's boyfriend of two years, said he appreciates that the police are interviewing everyone they can. "I was happy to be interviewed, and I hope everyone who knows something will speak up."

Mayor Colin Woods, Max Woods' father, said in a statement, "I hope for the sake of Claire and her family that they won't rule out anyone until all evidence is uncovered."

The Sangway Tribune *attempted to contact Gillman multiple times prior to publication of this story. Reached once by phone, he declined to comment.*

The investigation is ongoing.

Abby stared at the report as thoughts swam back and forth through her mind like a school of frightened fish. They would turn to wondering, and then to suspicion, and then to denial, over and over. Her head felt heavy, and she bristled when she felt a tear try to leak from her eye.

Nothing in the story said Uncle Keith was involved. The police didn't think he was. The dockman confirmed he was on Blueberry Island when Claire was believed to have disappeared, and that he was alone.

But why had they met that night? Why were they meeting in a diner? Abby couldn't imagine meeting any of her teachers for dinner. She felt weird enough when she accidentally ran into them at Target or the grocery store, like they were actors onstage at the wrong time. Maybe high school was different. Maybe Uncle Keith's meetings with Claire were different.

The only person who seemed to be saying so, though, was Claire's boyfriend. Abby recognized his name in the article and knew he'd been one of the boys she overheard on the wharf. Maybe Max was just jealous of Uncle Keith. Maybe Max had bad grades and was mad at him. Maybe he was just upset that his girlfriend was missing.

The two sides of the story rammed in Abby's mind. She didn't know what to think, and the only person she wanted to tell her the truth had declined to comment. Even Aunt Sandra had confirmed what time he was home. Couldn't Uncle Keith have said anything to the reporter? "Declined to comment" sounded even guiltier than "It was me."

Abby's brain didn't have an answer to that—which only made her feel worse. She got up and wandered from her room in a daze. She stayed upstairs—the last thing she needed was to be near the basement—and walked down the hall.

A small streak of light from the afternoon sun jutted across her path. The door to her uncle's room was open.

Abby stood in the doorway and took it in as she had when she'd first arrived. The guitar still leaned against the bookshelf, the comforter was still rumpled, and there were still dirty socks and shirts on the floor. Abby rolled her eyes and breathed a laugh as she stepped into the room. Her mother often clucked about how men were a mess and how she was grateful for a daughter. Abby wasn't aware of her father's messes, but if he was anything like Uncle Keith, her mother had her work cut out for her.

A circle of green amongst the dirty socks stopped Abby in her tracks. She studied the piece of clothing on the floor. The green revealed itself to be Keroppi, a cartoon frog she'd seen staring at her from the window at the Hello Kitty store at the mall. Now Keroppi stared at her from the center of a small pair of white panties.

Abby's heart and skin turned to ice as she backed away. Those panties looked like they belonged to a teenage girl.

CHAPTER 10

"You're pretty quiet tonight, Skipper."

Abby looked up from stirring her pasta. Uncle Keith had brought back something special, as promised: meatballs from an Italian butcher close to the mainland, where he and Aunt Sandra used to buy meat when she'd visit them. Abby had only managed a small smile when Uncle Keith presented them.

Making matters worse was the small flash of hurt in Uncle Keith's eyes when Abby was less than enthusiastic about the meatballs. "Well, maybe they'll be more exciting once they're cooked," he'd said.

"I'm sure they'll be great," Abby said as Uncle Keith walked into the kitchen. "Thanks." Guilt swam through her veins, and she considered just asking Uncle Keith about the article, and even what she'd overheard on the wharf. Then she pictured him getting upset that she didn't trust him—or worse still, confirming that things with Claire weren't as innocent as Chloe had said.

Left unchallenged though, her suspicions took the chance to manifest. Max's accusations, along with the Keroppi panties in Uncle Keith's room, swirled in a storm that conjured up Uncle Keith having dinner with a teenage student, casting jealous looks at her boyfriend and refusing to talk to the paper about his involvement or lack thereof. Then she felt guilty for ever thinking those things about Uncle Keith, and think that maybe she should ask him to calm her fears. Then it would start all over again, a cycle that left her frightened, angry, and sad—not to mention mute.

"Are you okay?" Uncle Keith asked as he speared a meatball.

Abby nodded, and hoped her sadness, at least, stayed in her throat along with her meal.

"Did you have fun at the house today?" Uncle Keith paused to chew and swallow. "Did you do any work? Maybe paint that bathroom?"

"No," Abby muttered. "Why would I do that alone?"

Uncle Keith lost his smile. "I only asked because you said you might do some work alone this afternoon. I don't expect you to."

"I didn't get a chance."

"Well, you will tomorrow. I have tomorrow off—I made sure of it. Maybe we can tackle the upstairs."

Yes, upstairs, away from the basement and all of Uncle Keith's secrets—except for the one in his room. Abby speared her last meatball with a bit of extra force.

"Are you sure you're—"

"Yes. I'm fine." Abby couldn't stay at the table, not while her mind was going in all sorts of directions. "Thank you for dinner," she said as she stood up. "The meatballs were very good." They'd tasted like any old meatballs, but Abby didn't want to leave without acknowledging his act of kindness. Even knowing what he might've done, she still wanted to be kind to him. Why? What was wrong with her?

"Thanks," Uncle Keith said. "If you feel better later, come downstairs and we'll watch a movie."

"Okay."

"And we're spending the day together tomorrow. I promise."

Did you promise Claire she'd be able to get away? Did she break a promise to you?

"See you," Abby said. She darted out of the kitchen and went upstairs.

Abby stayed in her room for the rest of the evening. She listened to the waves outside and tried to focus on them instead of her swirling thoughts. An hour or so after dinner, she heard music between the crash and pull of the ocean. It sounded like a guitar.

She glanced out the window and saw Uncle Keith sitting by himself on the porch, a bottle of beer on the table and his guitar in his lap. Abby remembered their Gillman Crew nights, where she'd sit with a soda while he sat with a beer, and he'd play songs for both of them to sing along to.

The chords sounded nice—Uncle Keith hadn't lost his talent—but the sight of him playing alone made Abby's heart heavy. She briefly considered looking for a soda in the fridge and joining him outside.

A final image of the panties flashed across her mind, one strong enough to harden her heart once more. Maybe with everything he'd done, and everything he wouldn't comment on, he deserved to sit outside alone.

Abby woke up the next morning feeling slightly better, though her mood worsened with each waking memory of the day before fluttering into her brain. She hoped that working on the house would take her mind off things, or at least, have her and Uncle Keith be too busy to talk to each other beyond tools and paint.

When Abby walked into the kitchen, she saw Uncle Keith in a puffy red vest and what looked like new jeans. "Aren't you worried about getting paint on those clothes?" Abby asked.

Uncle Keith jumped a little and set down his coffee. "What, no good morning before you worry about my clothes?" he said with a smile.

"Are you working today?" Abby said as feelings of both dread and relief fought for dominance in her mind.

"Nope. I promised you I'd be home, and I'm keeping that promise."

"Then why aren't you—"

"It's a nice day out." Abby looked out the window and saw nothing but grey skies. Uncle Keith clarified, "It's not going to rain, but the clouds'll scare off a lot of the tourists. I thought I'd take us out for a ride."

Abby perked up for the first time in twenty-four hours. "On your boat?"

"Yeah. We'll get some work done later, but we can take a spin around the water, maybe circle the islands …"

Abby thought of Blueberry Island, and memories of the day before dashed the good mood she was beginning to have.

"But it'll be nice. We'll go right after breakfast."

Abby didn't want to argue. Uncle Keith seemed determined, and any hesitations she had weren't ones she wanted to share with him. "Sure. Sounds good," she said with a nod. Uncle Keith smiled, but Abby headed straight to the bag of bagels on the counter.

They shared a small breakfast with smaller talk. Soon, they walked along the beach towards the docks. Abby saw the dead counselor walking along the dunes. She looked towards Abby and her uncle, but thankfully kept her distance. Abby averted her gaze as soon as she saw the first tendril of flayed skin begin to curl.

"Morning Keith!"

Abby looked towards the docks and saw a black man with a sailor's cap and silver beard walking towards them. She saw "Lucas" stitched in gold cursive on his jacket. Abby blanched as she remembered Lucas' quotes from the story about Uncle Keith.

"Hey Luke." Uncle Keith and Lucas slapped each other on the back as they gave a quick hug, just like Uncle Keith had done with her father. Abby thought again how painful it must be for men to be nice to each other.

"You both going for a ride?" he asked.

"Yeah, figured we'd take advantage of everyone thinking it's going to rain."

"Well, you know the usual: be careful, and don't let me see you not putting your life jacket on." Lucas chuckled before turning to return to his booth. Abby wanted to ask him about the article, and wished they could chat a little longer while Uncle Keith prepared the boat.

"Abby? This way."

Uncle Keith nodded from further down the dock towards his boat. It was the same speedboat she remembered, white all over except for flecks of algae and age in the paint, with *Listen to the Sea* painted in navy cursive letters on the side. Two seats sat up front, with only a trunk in the back. She'd have to sit next to him. She'd probably have to talk to him.

Abby took a deep breath, then picked up her gait. She would've had to do those things eventually, and now was a good a time as any.

———

Even if Abby had wanted to talk right away, there was no chance of Uncle Keith hearing her. The engine roared as they sped away from the dock. Abby couldn't help but smile at the wind in her face and the occasional spray of mist from the ocean as the boat crossed the waves. Soon the shore was a faint tan strip, and her grandparents' house a shadow against the sky.

"Where are we going?" Abby shouted.

"Just around!" Uncle Keith shouted back. He circled away from Crane's Despot, then slowed down the engine, bringing its roar to a hum. He steered the boat in a steady path between the islands.

"I thought just being out on the water, instead of hiking around, would be nice," Uncle Keith said as he sat back. "Give us a peaceful place to talk."

Abby whipped her head to Uncle Keith. "Talk about what?" she asked.

"Anything. The weather, school—"

Abby relaxed.

"And you know—just everything that's been going on."

Abby felt the familiar cold of dread begin to creep up her skin. She knew she couldn't spend the entire week avoiding this talk, and she certainly couldn't now, when they were in a boat and miles away from anyone else. Was he trapping her? Did he know she knew too much?

Abby shook her head. She was going crazy.

"I know something's bothering you, Skipper," Uncle Keith said. "You have a lot of talents, but acting isn't one of them."

Abby managed a small laugh.

"But, I also know the last thing teens want to talk about is what's bothering them. Hell, your dad and I made it a point to talk about anything but that. He'd tell me to save the tears for my diary."

Abby furrowed her brow. "That doesn't sound like Dad. He listens to me."

"Well yeah, you're his daughter. And maybe your mom's helped him out some, but—well, our parents wanted us to stay strong and keep a stoic face forward, even when things got hard. Where we lived, though, made it pretty hard to do that sometimes." Uncle Keith nodded toward Blueberry Island. "It's one of the reasons we moved out to Phillip's Glen before I started middle school. It was just too much for the family to stay here."

"Is that why you don't like talking about the murders?" Abby asked. "And why you got so mad about that book?"

"Partly, but hey, that's got nothing to do with you. Can't imagine how a horrible event from before you were born would bother you."

If he only knew. Uncle Keith gave Abby a playful tap on her shoulder. She didn't smile. She stayed quiet, knowing

Uncle Keith would never believe she'd seen the four dead kids and their counselor.

"But I think I know what's bothering you," Uncle Keith continued.

"Really? What?"

"Aunt Sandra being gone."

Abby suppressed a snort. True, she missed Aunt Sandra; but she'd been the farthest thing from Abby's mind for the past two days.

"And me being gone."

"You?"

"Yeah. I haven't seen you in four years." Uncle Keith looked at her with such remorse that Abby briefly forgot her suspicions. "I've been busy, and so have you."

Busy? Abby hadn't been busy. It was always Uncle Keith who hadn't wanted her to come to Sangway Bluff until now—and even then, it was just to help work on the house. Something they hadn't done because, until this morning, Uncle Keith had been away at the bookstore.

"But that doesn't excuse me not coming to see you, or trying harder to work out you coming to visit us."

"No," Abby spat. "It doesn't."

Uncle Keith's mouth dropped, and Abby blanched. Before she could backtrack, Uncle Keith regained his composure and nodded. "No, you're right," he said. "It doesn't, and you have every right to say that to me."

"Thanks. I do." The wave of comfort she'd gotten from Uncle Keith not yelling at her quickly bubbled into frustration that begged to be released. "I should be able to say to you that I wanted to come all those summers. I wanted to, but you and Dad told me I couldn't. I didn't even hear from you the past two years."

"Hey, I called—"

"Just to say happy birthday. I almost started to forget what Sangway Bluff looked like. I loved coming here. It was almost like a magic place for me." A place that was now ruined by ghosts in the basement and allegations in an article. Abby bit her lip.

"I know, sweetie, and I'm sorry."

"For what? For forgetting that maybe I wanted to see you? For forgetting that we're family, and I'm not some obligation for you while Mom and Dad go places over the summer?"

"Hey, I never felt that way. Don't ever think that."

"And then you bring me back so I can help repair a house, a house that doesn't even have my aunt in it anymore because she left you—" Uncle Keith flinched, but Abby couldn't stop—"and which you're never in because you're too busy working—"

"I can't help that—"

"And too busy dodging reporters so you don't have to talk about Claire?"

Uncle Keith glared at her. Abby stopped, and while her heart thudded, she kept her gaze steady.

"What have you been reading?" Uncle Keith asked, his voice low and even.

He knew. Of course he knew—and his reaction only broke Abby's heart even more.

"Is it something you don't want me to read?" Abby asked. "Something you're hiding?"

Uncle Keith spun around and revved up the engine. "We're going home," he said before the engine drowned him out.

"Why won't you tell me the truth?" Abby shouted over the roar. Uncle Keith ignored her, but she could tell by how stiff he held his posture that he could hear her. "Why won't you talk to me about Claire? What do you have to hide?"

"I'm not hiding anything!"

"I saw the article in the Sangway Tribune! And I saw Claire's panties in your room!"

"What the hell? I don't have anything of hers, and definitely not those!"

"I saw them! Don't lie to me!"

"What were you doing in my room?"

"You won't comment on it in the paper and you won't talk to me! Why?"

"It has nothing to do with you!"

"Yes it does! You're my uncle, my blood relative, someone I love and admire! How do you think it feels to find out your uncle was involved with a missing teenager?"

Uncle Keith slowed the boat to a stop. He turned and glared at Abby. She shrank under his gaze.

"It probably feels the same as when your niece accuses you of being involved," he said.

Abby folded her arms. Even if she wanted to say anything, she wouldn't be able to. Her throat was choked with anger and disappointment.

Uncle Keith turned and revved the engine once more. "We're going home," Uncle Keith said as they sailed towards the dock. "And I'm calling your dad. I think they should come pick you up early."

Abby stayed silent, and watched the water as they pulled up closer to shore. She didn't want to go home, but she also knew the longer she stayed with Uncle Keith, the worse things would get.

They docked the boat and walked towards the beach without a word. Lucas waved from his station, and Uncle Keith gave a perfunctory wave back. Abby ignored him.

Once they were out of Lucas' earshot, Uncle Keith added, "I'm also going to talk to your dad about your attitude."

Abby stopped and sneered as she turned to face him. "What? You're going to tell on me like a little kid?"

"I will when you're acting like one."

"For God's sake. You and Chloe and everyone else keep telling me I'm acting like a little kid when I refuse to put up with your shit. I'm not a little kid and I'm not acting like one."

"A little kid pouts and screams instead of talking things out, and that's what you're doing."

"Oh, you want me to keep talking things out? Because it went so well out by the islands! First I bring up an article you don't want to talk about—"

"Abby—"

"What do you want me to talk about instead? The house we're not working on? The dead kids in the basement? What?!"

Uncle Keith's eyes shot to the size of quarters. Abby dropped her hands and felt a flush creep up her neck. Her seeing the ghosts had just popped out, but now, Uncle Keith had everything he needed to write her off as crazy. Abby looked down at her shoes, wishing she could scuttle under the beach like the clams he used to show her by dragging his toe along the wet sand.

"You mean the kids from Blueberry Island?"

Abby was about to mutter that of course that was who she meant, when she realized she'd only said dead kids. She hadn't told him who they were.

Abby looked up at Uncle Keith. His eyes were still wide, but they were filled with a heartbreaking combination of sadness and hopefulness.

"You see them too?"

CHAPTER 11

"It started when I was eleven."

Uncle Keith twirled a beer bottle in his hands ("I know it's early, but it'll be my only one," he'd said) and looked out over the deck as he spoke. Abby sat beside him and sipped a soda as she watched the waves and listened.

"I was sitting in my room," Uncle Keith continued. "I was reading a comic book, and I thought I saw something move across the rug. I was used to my periphery playing tricks on me, flickers of shadows and light, but this shadow stuck around. I looked up and saw Felicity."

Abby's eyes widened. "One of the Blueberry Island victims?"

"Yeah. Your dad used to go that camp. He was there when the murders happened—he was thirteen, but he'd gone every year since he was ten. That's how he met Felicity. She was his girlfriend."

Abby's eyes widened with each sentence, and her mouth dropped on the last. "Jesus! Are you going to tell me Mary's my long-lost aunt next?"

Uncle Keith laughed. "I know it's a lot. Our parents tried not to talk about it. Mom and Dad wanted your dad to move on. But you can't just ask someone to move on from that, especially a kid. It didn't hit me as something more than scary—I was just eight, after all—but I could sense how much it affected your dad. He kept his feelings inside, just like our parents wanted him to, but …"

Uncle Keith shrugged, and Abby asked, "Do you think that's why Felicity came back? So she could be remembered?"

"I have no idea. She didn't try to talk to me, and I was too scared the first time I saw her to talk to her. I thought I was seeing things, that I was crazy, the usual. But I started seeing people that weren't Felicity. People who were unnoticed by everyone else around me, people that gave me a feeling that they didn't belong with the living."

"I get that feeling too. Well, it's more like a coldness. Like a quick breeze—"

"Or a quick shudder up your spine? That's what I get."

"I don't get a shudder, but I almost always see blood."

"Huh. I don't see blood, unless it's on the person."

"Really? You've got blood trickling down the front of the house. You don't see it at all?" Abby pointed over the porch, where four faint lines trickled down the sand. Uncle Keith shook his head.

"Nope. I wouldn't have moved back in if I'd seen that." Uncle Keith chuckled, and Abby joined him. Even without that shared vision, Abby felt immense relief at being able to talk to someone about what she'd seen and not have them tell her she hadn't seen it.

"I'm surprised you stayed moved in after seeing the kids in the basement," Abby said.

"I just stayed out of the basement. It's one of the reasons I've put off renovating. I'd have to clear out those old boxes while four dead kids screamed at the walls and slashed their throats."

"So they don't talk to you either? I thought it was just me."

"It's not just you. But the weird part is that it didn't start that way."

"So they did talk to you?" Abby tried not to feel insulted.

"Well, not conversations or anything, but they didn't actively ignore me or move away like they do now. It started after—"

Uncle Keith swallowed, and Abby knit her brow.

"It started after Laura died," Uncle Keith said. He took a swig of beer.

Abby's brow softened as she remembered her father's story. "The girl who killed herself outside of Locker 751?" she asked.

Uncle Keith gave her a sad smile. "So your dad told you some things, I guess."

"Yeah. He told me about her when I first told him I saw a ghost. He was worried I'd start getting paranoid and hurt myself if I kept thinking I was seeing things. But I'm not just seeing things, and you're proof. I wish he could see that—I hated seeing him look at me like I was crazy when I told him. I hated how much I scared him."

"It's something that especially bothers your dad. You know Mary, the counselor? All the campers said she used to tell the best ghost stories. It was because she believed in them—but she was also afraid of them. It's why she hurt those kids."

"So you think it was Mary and not some other murderer?"

Uncle Keith narrowed his eyes. "You read that hack book, didn't you?"

Abby looked down at her soda, and Uncle Keith said, "It's okay. I should've known better than to make such a big deal about it. Of course you'd want to read it."

"But it was Mary?"

"Yes. Her fingerprints were on the knife they found at the scene. It was a murder-suicide. She didn't leave a note, but her best friend—one of the counselors—told the newspaper that her fear of ghosts on the islands was getting out of hand in the days leading up to the murder. She kept telling stories about malevolent spirits disturbing the islands and leering at her and the kids. One of her best-known stories was about the Clockmaker, an obsessive ghost who'd steal your digits—fingers, toes, bones—to make a clock if you weren't careful. They made her stop telling the story when she started getting really graphic about how those clocks were built and what the living had to do to stop the Clockmaker, but, well, you read about how they were found, right? It was right out of one of her stories."

"So, what, she was sacrificing the kids?"

"And herself. Again, all guessing; but it's an explanation that your dad took to heart. The fact that anyone was murdered, but especially his girlfriend, took a huge toll on him; and because it happened due to this counselor being obsessed with ghosts—"

"Then he wouldn't be happy with anyone saying they see ghosts."

"You got it. I never told your dad directly, but once I just suggested that some people could really see the dead, just to test the waters. He snapped, Abby. He screamed at me, told me it wasn't real, and that even entertaining the idea was dangerous. I knew better than to bring it up again."

"Yeah. It sucks not being able to talk to anyone about it—until now."

"That's how I felt when I met Laura."

Uncle Keith twirled his beer bottle in his hands and kept his eyes on the label. Abby waited a few moments, then gently nudged him by asking, "Was she your girlfriend, like Dad and Felicity?"

"No. But she believed me. She believed that people could see ghosts. She told me after class one day that she sensed something different about me, could feel a coldness coming from me and see a faint glow. She asked if I'd ever seen the dead amongst the living. I hadn't brought that up with anyone since your father, and David was in twelfth grade then—he wouldn't have spoken to Laura. She was asking me unprompted, so I told her I did. She believed me, and didn't judge me, and it felt so good. We became really close, so close that your dad was suspicious. He said he didn't like how invested she was in stuff that wasn't true."

"Stuff he didn't think was true."

"Right, but in some respects, he had a point. Laura was convinced there was a ghost in Locker 751. She was so convinced that she kept asking me to come with her to the school at night and hold a séance. She thought my presence would encourage the ghost of the dead girl to show herself. But I knew nothing was going to happen."

"Why?"

"Because that ghost doesn't exist. The Legend of Locker 751 is just that: a legend."

Abby's heart broke at Uncle Keith not believing her. "But I saw the ghost!" she insisted. "She was the first ghost I saw."

"There wasn't a ghost there. I never saw one, never had the shudder—"

"I saw blood trickling out of that locker. I saw a girl in there with gouged-out eyes. She hissed at me and kept banging her head against the locker. Maybe she's like the blood, maybe I can see her and you can't—"

"What did she look like?"

"Huh?"

Uncle Keith still didn't seem to believe her, but the sadness in his eyes tempered her frustration. "What did she look like?" Uncle Keith asked. "Apart from the gouged-out eyes?"

"I don't know. Dead. Young. A girl." She'd been so scared that she hadn't taken the time to process all of the ghost's features—not to mention the fact that she'd turned her back on Abby almost immediately.

Uncle Keith stood up and motioned towards the house. He walked inside and Abby followed, until she saw him walking towards the basement door.

"Why do we have to go down there?" Abby asked as the trails of blood appeared on the wood.

"I want to show you Laura," Uncle Keith replied. He opened the door and walked downstairs. Abby hesitated, then trotted behind him. It would be okay with Uncle Keith, someone else who could see what was downstairs.

As soon as Uncle Keith turned on the light, the four dead children scurried towards the walls. They hissed and roared and slashed their throats.

Uncle Keith walked straight to the boxes. "Oh, shut up!" he yelled as he pulled one out from a stack on the left. Abby couldn't help but smirk.

Uncle Keith set the box on the floor and used his keys to cut the strip of tape holding it closed. Abby peered inside and saw stacks of musty yearbooks. Uncle Keith dug, then pulled one out from Abby's middle school. She recognized the ram mascot, though it looked more cartoonish and was blazoned in silver.

The campers continued to roar, but it was easier to dismiss them as white noise. Uncle Keith flipped through the pages, then stopped and turned the yearbook towards Abby.

Abby faced a photo of a young girl, no more than twelve or thirteen. She wore a black blouse with a Peter Pan collar, one free of blood stains. She had a pixie cut that ended above her ears. Her eyes stared straight at Abby, wide and present; but Abby could practically see the holes and blood she'd seen staring back at her from Locker 751.

"This is who you saw," Uncle Keith said. He didn't need to ask—Abby was sure her face told him what he suspected. Even so, Abby nodded, her eyes glued to the last school photo of Laura Pennington.

CHAPTER 12

Abby and Uncle Keith moved back upstairs, but sat at the kitchen table instead of the porch. His beer bottle empty, he switched to soda.

"I thought for sure it was the girl in the legend," Abby said. "I thought she'd had her eyes gouged out and Laura mimicked her."

"Laura killed herself, but everything after that's just conjecture. Kind of like the legend itself. It always changes, but that's because it isn't true. It's easy to manipulate a story whose only purpose is to scare kids, and that's what the Legend of Locker 751 was: a way the eighth graders scared sixth graders."

"Not anymore. I never knew there was a Legend of Locker 751 until Dad mentioned it."

"I'm sure he'd rather you think you were scared by a legend than actually seeing a dead girl. He would've thought you were going to be like Mary."

"He was afraid I'd become like Laura."

"And I'm not surprised by that." Uncle Keith took a long sip of his soda. "Your dad caught me getting ready to sneak out to see Laura," he said. "On the night she died, I mean."

"I thought you didn't believe her that there was a ghost."

"I didn't. I knew there wasn't. I hoped that by finally going, though, I could convince her that it was just a legend and there weren't any tortured spirits living in her locker. But your dad told me not to go. He said there was no convincing people like Laura, that she was troubled and I would be endangering myself. He practically begged me not to go—and he's way more convincing when he's afraid than when he's angry."

Abby remembered how the fear in her father's eyes had convinced her not to protest what she'd seen any further. It seemed her father had had a similar effect on both her and her uncle.

"And when she killed herself, it seemed he was proven right. But I can't help but think it would've been different if I'd just gone. I could've helped her, tried to talk her down from her imagination. But I left her alone and scared, and I guess she couldn't take it."

Uncle Keith's voice caught a little as he spoke. Abby looked at him with pity. "It's not your fault," she said. "We've been learning about that in school, how as sad as it is, it's never a friend or family member's fault when someone commits suicide."

"I know it's not my fault, but I can't help it, you know? She helped me feel better about what I saw. I could've done the same. I just wanted to help her." His voice trailed into just above a whisper as he looked away. "It's what I wanted—"

He stopped speaking, but Abby felt a completion of his sentence in her mind. "It's what you wanted for Claire?" she asked.

Uncle Keith stared at the table for a moment, then nodded.

"Was she like Laura? Or was she like you? Like us, I mean?"

"No, nothing like that."

"So, you were helping her with school, or—"

"Can we please not talk about Claire?"

Abby's shoulders slumped. "You know what was really bothering me about everything with Claire, Uncle Keith? That you wouldn't talk about it."

Uncle Keith looked at her. He didn't look angry, and he didn't say anything. Abby decided to keep going while she still felt brave.

"Yes, you told me she was missing. And yes, I read that article in the Sangway Tribune. I'm sorry. Carmen found it and she sent it to me. I also overheard Claire's boyfriend on the wharf—"

Uncle Keith straightened like soldier on command. "You talked to Max?"

"No, I just—"

"Did he talk to you?"

"No! I only heard him talking to his friend. But they were talking about Claire and they talked about you."

Uncle Keith relaxed, but his expression remained dark. "Of course they were," he muttered.

"And maybe it wasn't fair of me to assume anything was wrong between you and Claire—"

"Nothing was wrong."

"But you won't tell me what was right! You won't tell anyone, not even the paper. You wouldn't comment further."

"I didn't comment further because I promised Claire that I wouldn't. It's a promise I didn't want to break. My reputation wasn't worth sacrificing that."

"I don't know what any of that means, though, because you won't say anything to me! Can you please tell me what happened? I've been able to talk about what I've been seeing with you and it's felt so great. You can trust me, Uncle Keith. You can talk to me about it. I won't tell anyone."

Uncle Keith sighed and rubbed his eyes. Abby slumped in her chair, convinced that no matter what she said or how much she pleaded, Claire's story would remain locked in Uncle Keith's conscious.

"It wasn't worth breaking that promise when the article was written," he said.

Abby glanced up at Uncle Keith. He too sat slumped, his eyes sad but locked on hers. They looked like defeated mirrors of each other, worn by secrets kept.

"The police questioned me a couple weeks after she went missing," Uncle Keith continued. "I knew she'd run away. I was the only one who knew."

Abby felt a hundred questions leap into her throat. She swallowed them. She didn't want to start interrogating him and scare him back into silence.

"She told me in the diner that night that she was going to run away. She was running away from Max."

"Max? Why?

Uncle Keith folded his arms. "Max was always just enough of an asshole to scare Claire but no one else. Even her parents didn't see it. Cynthia is friends with Mayor

Woods, and Mayor Woods is really popular around here. Made it easy for Max to make Claire think she'd have no one on her side."

"But you were, right?"

"Of course I was. I know abusive assholes when I see them. You don't live with someone like your grandpa and come away with nothing." Uncle Keith snorted as he sipped his soda. "I always thought Max seemed like a jerk," he continued. "But I didn't start to see it until Claire started staying after school with me for our enriched reading program. I've done that with lots of students, not just Claire. Readers who want more than just the syllabus. Separate books and projects, with one-on-one tutoring. The school always knew about it, and Claire's parents knew I was meeting with her. It was completely fine."

"And it was like that with all your students, right?" Abby asked, as an image of the Keroppi panties flashed across her mind.

"Yes, Abby. Look at me."

Abby fixed her gaze on Uncle Keith.

"I promise you that I've never done anything wrong with any of my students," he said. "I really need you to believe me."

Abby did her best to block out the image of the underwear. She also tried to nod. Instead, she said, "I just can't stop thinking about those panties I saw on your floor."

"Well, aside from the fact that you shouldn't have been snooping around in my room, I can assure you they belong to an adult. Now, can we please stop talking about this? This is the last thing I want to talk about with my niece."

Abby nodded. "Okay. I believe you."

"Thanks." Uncle Keith sighed as he leaned back in his chair. "Well, Claire would meet with me after school, but Max was always hovering in the doorway. Not the whole time, but he'd show up earlier and earlier. He'd want to sit in and he'd constantly interrupt, trying to get Claire to leave early. He wanted her to spend all her time with him. I could tell she didn't like it. She'd jump when he came in and said hey. She always looked a little afraid before she'd turn to face him. She loved him, but she never seemed happy to see him when he showed up like that."

"Well, even if I loved him, I wouldn't want that person in my face all the time."

"No, and you shouldn't. That's not love, that's obsession and control. That's what Max was doing. He wanted to control Claire. He wanted her to do the same extracurriculars with him, read the same books, go to the same college—"

"He wanted to go to Brown?"

"No. He's going to Boston College, and he wanted Claire to go too. Claire never wanted that. She wanted options outside of the state. She'd lived here her whole life. She wanted to explore. She'd been looking at out-of-state colleges since tenth grade. Sandra and I both wrote her letters of recommendation for Brown. She should've been ecstatic about getting in, but when she told me she got in, she was afraid. She said Max wasn't happy. She hoped he'd feel better as the year went on, but—"

Uncle Keith shrugged, and Abby did too. "So did you guys start going to the diner to start plotting her escape?"

"No. We started going there because Claire wanted to be somewhere Max couldn't corner her after school. She also figured he'd be less inclined to make a scene in front of an entire diner."

"He didn't mind making a scene in front of you."

"And if it came down to it, he would've made a scene in public too. Despite her growing fears, though, Claire still loved him. She wanted to believe he'd change, that he'd see things and give her the same leeway that she constantly gave him." Uncle Keith leaned forward. "Abby, please listen to me when I say that guys like that will never change. If you're ever feeling controlled, possessed, or afraid of anyone you're dating, please, get out of it and get out early. Someone who truly loves you will never make you feel those things. They don't love you, they love their power over you. Okay?"

"Were you really that afraid of Max?"

"Claire was, in the end. The night she left, Claire emailed me and asked if we could meet earlier to discuss our book. But she didn't have her book when she arrived. She told me that she and Max had had a fight earlier that day, and he'd said he'd rather she be dead than going to another school. He tried to write it off as a joke, but Claire wasn't convinced. She told me she was going to run away before it could escalate. She had this elaborate plan to get far away, to disappear and make it seem like she was gone."

"She told you, though."

"Yeah. She knew I had no kind feelings towards Max, and I was also the least connected to him or his family. She wanted someone to know, because her plan was to get in touch with me once she felt safe and to deliver a message to Cynthia and Maureen that she was okay. She'd figure something out with Brown, with her parents, always stuff to be figured out. She'd get to it. I tried to get her to stay a little longer before she left, to think things through more, even to go to the police about Max, but she wouldn't have it. She'd made her decision, and she asked me to promise her I wouldn't tell anyone she'd run away, not until I heard from her; so that she could disappear and be safe. That's why I didn't comment. She was still missing when they wrote that article."

"But she's still missing now. You said yourself that she disappeared. I know a lot of people assume she's dead, but that's what she wanted, right?"

"Yeah, but—"

"Then she could still be out there. Maybe it's just taking a while. Maybe you'll hear from her soon and everything will be okay."

"It won't, Abby. Claire's dead."

"How do you know?" The question shot the answer into Abby's brain as soon as she asked it. Abby watched in mortified silence as Uncle Keith brought his fists to his eyes. His knuckles were soon covered in tears, and his shoulders began to shake.

"Where did you see her?" Abby asked as gently as possible.

"In class." The answer came sputtering out on the heels of a sob. "She was sitting in her old desk. I didn't notice at first. I was taking attendance and going down the names and marked her as there. But then I remembered she was gone, and I looked at her again, and—"

Uncle Keith cried into his hands. Abby sat frozen, unsure of what to do. She'd never seen a grown man cry before.

"I'm sorry," Uncle Keith said as he wiped his eyes. "I don't want to put this all on you, but—"

"It's okay," Abby assured him.

"It's not. You're a kid, you don't need this."

"But if you can't talk to me, who can you talk to this about? Who else will believe that you saw her?"

"That's the problem! That's why I can't comment to anyone now. They already suspected me before. How's it going to sound if I tell them I know she's dead because I saw her ghost in my classroom?" Uncle Keith gulped down another sob and leaned back. His eyes were bright red. "It was bad enough that I lost it in front of my students. I couldn't teach that day, and I couldn't tell any of them what was wrong, because—"

Uncle Keith broke down in sobs again, and Abby clutched his wrist. "You can talk to me. I can handle it, really."

Uncle Keith took two deep breaths, then nodded. "That's why I was let go," Uncle Keith said, though Abby suspected as much. "I didn't cry, but it was bad. I just crumpled at my desk and couldn't stop screaming. I was already sick of seeing dead students wander in and out of the school. Old ghosts, kids I'd never even met, all of them ignoring me; but no less awful to see. It's been awful seeing the dead. I didn't want this, even when they weren't so adamant about ignoring me. But that's all I ever seem to see: ghosts of people who were killed, or who killed themselves."

Abby remembered the people she'd seen. The boy in the cafeteria had run away from her before she could see any wounds, but Mayor Holden had had rope marks around his neck. The children in the basement had slashed throats. And Laura …

"That's all I seem to see too," she said. "People who shouldn't have died, and who're sticking around anyway."

"Yeah. I don't think I've seen anyone that died from natural causes. But seeing the students was always the hardest. You never want to see someone so young and know that they're dead." He began to weep again. "And I never, ever wanted to see Claire like that!"

Uncle Keith leaned into his arm and cried. Abby stood up and walked to his side of the table. She reached down and hugged him. Uncle Keith didn't move, but his crying seemed to soften under her hold.

"And I don't even know what happened to her," Uncle Keith said after a few moments. He sat up and squeezed Abby's wrist. She stayed standing next to him. "I know she won't tell me, and no one's found her body yet. With every day she's gone, she's just another kid who disappeared. I know she's dead. You believe she's dead—"

"I know she's dead. I believe you."

"But what good is us knowing—us seeing people like Claire and Felicity and all the others—if they won't even speak to us?"

Abby shrugged. "I mean, everyone we've seen is someone who died too early. Maybe they're pissed that we can see them, but there's nothing we can do to bring them back."

Uncle Keith leaned back in his chair. "I just wish I knew why," he whispered.

He could've meant a host of things, but Abby didn't feel the need to ask. She felt the weight of his emotions on her heart, and knew that in addition to their blood and their abilities, it would be something that they'd share. Perhaps it was that knowing that would be the only sense of comfort they could find.

"I know," Abby said. "Me too."

CHAPTER 13

Abby and Uncle Keith didn't get any work done on the house. The events of the morning led to a day spent watching movies, reading, and ordering pizza for dinner.

The next morning, Uncle Keith woke Abby up by gently shaking her. "What's up?" she asked.

"Betsy just called and needs a little extra help setting up for an event at the bookstore this afternoon. I won't be in all day, but I'll be in for a little bit."

"Okay," Abby said. She didn't mind. She'd accepted that work on the house was probably not going to happen this week.

"You want to come in with me? It'll only be about an hour or two."

"Sure." Abby sat up and got out of bed. "And I'll try not to read more of *Blueberry Hell*," Abby said with a smile.

Uncle Keith snorted, but didn't seem entirely happy with the joke. "I'll see you downstairs," he said as he left her room. Abby made a mental note to not even joke about the book, though she wondered how bad the author's conspiracies were that Uncle Keith hated them so much.

As they drove along the coastline towards the wharf, Abby stared out at Blueberry Island. The trees she could see were an unbroken, green line; lush and deep. Abby wondered how dark its woods were.

"Do you think anyone is on Blueberry Island?" Abby asked. "Anyone dead, I mean."

"There are a few. Mostly Native Americans, a couple Puritans. There's one who I think was a minister. He's always standing on a rock like he's about to preach." Uncle Keith chuckled under his breath. "With the look he gives me, I'm glad he won't talk to me."

"That's right, you've gone there recently. You were there when—"

Abby stopped herself, but Keith readily replied, "When Claire disappeared. Yup. I was there that night, with no one except the same old ghosts that are always there."

"Were you going to visit the ghosts?"

"Not necessarily. I go there to see if I can pick up anything about the murders. Some type of hint or vision. Deep down, I know it's fruitless; but I also feel better doing that than just ignoring the kids in the basement. Maybe if I get some answers, they won't be so angry."

"Maybe. But then they'd have to let you talk to them about those answers."

Uncle Keith laughed a little. "Maybe I can write it on a note and throw it downstairs."

Abby laughed as well, but didn't talk about it further. She was getting tired of saying maybe—she wanted actual answers.

"Morning guys!"

Abby stopped herself from plugging her ears at the sound of Chloe's voice. She waved from the front desk, which resulted in a rattling noise from Chloe's necklace striking the buttons on her jacket. "Good to see you again, Abby," she said with that extra octave that Abby couldn't stand.

"Hi," Abby replied, unable to muster up a convincing enough face to say it was good to see her too. Chloe put her arm down, and Abby saw quite the array of buttons: a *Bernie 2020* button, a skull with a flower over where the ear should be, Mickey Mouse with a nose ring. If they had never spoken, Abby might've thought Chloe was pretty cool.

The topmost button stopped Abby's journey across Chloe's jacket. Keroppi stared at her against a plain white background. Abby froze, and her eyes widened a little before she could stop them.

"Do I have something on me?" Chloe asked with a hesitant smile as she checked her jacket.

"No, no," Abby said as she snapped herself out of it. "I was just looking at your buttons."

"Oh! Yeah, I've collected a lot over the years. Here, check out the ones on the back." Chloe took off her jacket, revealing extensive tattooed sleeves on both arms. Abby took the jacket out of politeness, but could barely process its buttons. Instead, when Chloe turned back towards the cash register, Abby cast a questioning glare at Uncle Keith. Uncle Keith ignored her, but the scarlet color that ran up the back of his neck was more than enough confirmation of her suspicions.

"So, Betsy wrangled you in here for one more day, huh?" Chloe asked as she smiled at Uncle Keith.

"Just to help set up for the signing," Uncle Keith said. He rolled his eyes as he spoke. "There's no way in hell I'm staying for the whole thing."

"Who's coming?" Abby asked.

Before she could be answered, another woman's voice replied, "I know, Keith, you've made that clear."

Abby turned and saw an older woman walking towards them. She smiled as she approached them, but Abby could see even behind her glasses that her eyes were warning Uncle Keith not to argue further.

Uncle Keith gave a curt nod, then motioned towards Abby. "Betsy, this is my niece, Abby."

"Hi Abby." Betsy's greeting was warm and her expression softened as she held out her hand. Abby took it and smiled back. She liked the warmth she exuded.

"Well, thanks for coming in on short notice," Betsy said back to Keith. "I promise not to keep you here more than needed, but—"

"No problem. I'll help set up and then get going." He smiled at Abby as Betsy returned to her back office. "Want to help out, Skipper?"

"Sure!" Abby followed Uncle Keith towards the storeroom, grateful to not be left alone with Chloe. "You gonna pay me?"

"Twenty bucks an hour to start."

"Whoa, really? I was kidding."

"If this takes more than an hour, I'll be shocked." Uncle Keith hoisted one of two heavy boxes off of a cart and pulled a pocketknife out of his jeans.

"What are we doing?" Abby asked as Uncle Keith sliced through the packing tape on the box.

"Setting up for a book signing." Uncle Keith gave Abby a sardonic grin as he opened the box. "Your new favorite book, actually."

Abby furrowed her brow as she peered inside, then sighed when she saw several fresh copies of *Blueberry Hell*. "Look, I said I was sorry for reading it," she said.

"No worries, I was just teasing. But we need to bring these outside and stack them by the empty card table in the back of the store. Then we have to set up chairs and signs and stuff, and then we can go."

"Are that many people going to come?" Abby asked as she picked up a copy of the book.

"Oh yeah. They'll probably start lining up in the next hour or so." Uncle Keith picked up a large stack with a small grunt. "Me and Chloe might be the only people in the store who want nothing to do with this book, and even Chloe only feels that way because we're friends."

Abby was about to scoff at Uncle Keith referring to Chloe as just a friend, when he added, "But it's not our place to say. It's definitely not something to bring up too much." Uncle Keith nodded towards the wall behind Abby.

Abby turned and saw a closed door, which she presumed led to Betsy's office. She almost dropped her book. A trickle of blood seeped from underneath the doorway.

"Just bring the books out a few at a time," Uncle Keith said. He left, but Abby didn't follow. Instead, she moved towards Betsy's office.

The door was shut entirely. Abby couldn't see inside. She leaned towards the wood to see if she heard any sounds of distress, though in her heart, she knew it wasn't Betsy's blood that poured through the cracks. She wondered who was in there with her.

She rapped twice on the door. "Come in!" Betsy called.

Abby opened the door. Betsy's office was an office in the loosest sense of the term. It looked like a walk-in closet with a desk and a shelf. The streaming trickle stretched from the door towards Betsy's desk. However, Abby didn't see a ghost or any other person aside from Betsy.

"Hi Abby," Betsy said. "Does your uncle need something?"

"No, I—" Abby tried to think of a better excuse to be there than 'I saw blood seeping from your office and wanted to see which ghosts were here.' She said, "I was just wondering what it's like running a bookstore."

"Well, it's a lot of paperwork, a lot of ordering, and a lot of hoping we'll make money." Betsy chuckled a little as Abby walked closer to Betsy's desk. The trickle seemed to be coming from beneath a pile of papers. Abby wondered if a ghost could make themselves small.

"Your uncle's letting you read that book?" Betsy pointed at the copy of *Blueberry Hell* in Abby's hands.

"Oh. No. I'm helping him set up for the signing."

"Ah. Probably too grisly for you anyway."

Abby blinked as she saw an extra surge of blood seep from beneath the stack of papers.

"I know your uncle's not happy with it," Betsy continued. She grinned. "Hope he didn't send you in here to try and get me to cancel the signing."

"Oh no, I came in here on my own."

"Don't worry, I know."

"But is he the only one upset? He said a lot of the victims' families still live here. Aren't they upset too?"

"They haven't told me. And he can't play the family card against me. He knows that."

Betsy glanced at a photo on her desk. Abby saw a smiling teen girl in a white dress. Abby squinted, then tried not to jump when she realized she'd seen that same girl, but with flayed skin as she walked along the beach.

"I'm closer to it than he is," Betsy said, her voice soft.

"I'm sorry," Abby said sincerely. "Were you Mary's mother?"

"Aunt. But I loved her as much as I would my own child. She was wonderful. She told amazing stories, and had such a vivid imagination."

Too vivid, Abby thought; but fortunately, it stayed in her thoughts. "Won't having this signing—this book—be hard for you?" Abby asked instead.

Betsy's expression darkened. "No more than all the news coverage accusing my niece of being a murderer." She picked up the photo. "I know Mary had her problems, but it's ridiculous to say she killed those kids. That's just one story, though, and the one the cops chose to go with so they could close the case. Personally, I admire writers like this who are willing to look deeper, to try to find out who really did it."

Betsy moved the stack of papers. Abby saw a jade bowl, which held a silver whistle. The whistle rested in a pool of blood, which trickled down from the desk and onto the floor.

"This was Mary's," Betsy said as she picked it up. "She called it her ghost whistle, one that would scare away anything bad. When she became a counselor, she used it to scare off animals and anything dangerous. She used it to help kids. How could anyone think she would kill them?"

Abby didn't know. Abby couldn't say. She was too fixated on the blood from the whistle pooling onto Betsy's hands. The skin on her hands began to curl and flay like Mary's. Abby's eyes widened, then squinted as she saw what appeared to be letters forming through the blood. One word glowed all over Betsy's hand like scars through a wound: STAINED.

"I'm sorry about Mary," Abby said with a swallow. "I—I'm sure she thought she was helping—"

"Mary had her problems. She'd get scared like any other kid, especially one who's so imaginative. But she wouldn't kill kids in cold blood."

"I—"

"Just remember that sometimes, people go with what's sensation over common sense." Betsy set the whistle back down. The blood poured from her hands and into the bowl, where it pooled around the whistle before trickling over the sides. Her hand was clean, devoid of words and scars. "And it's okay to look at an old story from all angles, even if it hurts to open up those wounds again. I live with the wound of my niece being gone every day."

"Right. Well, I better finish helping Uncle Keith."

Betsy nodded. "Nice to meet you, Abby."

"You too." Abby shuffled out of the office without glancing back.

———

Abby was dying to tell Uncle Keith about what she'd seen in Betsy's office. Preparation for the signing, though, took a bit of time even with Abby helping; and Betsy asked Uncle Keith to help with a few other tasks before he was finally able to go.

"Okay, Skipper," Uncle Keith said with a sigh of relief as they exited the bookstore. "Let's head home and maybe, finally, get some work done on the house."

"I need to talk to you." Abby said as they walked past a small line of people gathered outside the bookstore.

"Sure. What about?"

"Back at the bookstore—"

"You can ask about anything except Chloe."

"Chloe? What about her?"

Uncle Keith glanced at her. "You weren't going to ask me about her?"

"No. Why would I?" Abby suddenly remembered the Keroppi button on Chloe's jacket, and looked down at the dock in embarrassment. "I don't care if she's your girlfriend," Abby said, mostly with sincerity. Chloe was annoying, but it wasn't like she was living with Uncle Keith or anything.

"She's not my girlfriend."

"Oh come on."

"No really, it's not—it's too soon for that. I don't want you thinking I'd just forget Sandra like that."

"I'm not thinking that. I don't care about you and Aunt Sandra." Uncle Keith looked hurt for a moment, and Abby added, "I mean, I care about Aunt Sandra, but you and her and Chloe aren't what I wanted to talk to you about."

"Oh. Then, what's up?"

"When I was in the backroom, I talked to—"

"Wait. Just a sec, Skipper."

Abby was about to protest, but Uncle Keith stopped and clutched her arm to stop her as well. She looked ahead in the same direction as Uncle Keith. A woman stood outside of the gourmet grocery store. She wore a blue apron with the name of the store written in cursive across the front. She had short brown hair and pearl earrings, and she smoked a cigarette with trembling hands. Her cheeks were wet.

"Maureen," Uncle Keith called.

The woman looked up. "Keith," she breathed. She dropped the cigarette, crushed it out with her foot, and walked towards them, though she barely noticed Abby. "Cynthia just called me," she said, her voice more choked with every word. "The police just called her. They …"

She broke into a sob, and Uncle Keith wrapped his arms around her. She began to cry into his shoulder. Abby watched with confusion, repeating the names Maureen and Cynthia in her brain until the vague familiarity clicked into a memory: they were Claire's parents.

Maureen's crying grew louder with each second. Uncle Keith rocked her and patted her back. Through her cries, Abby could discern a phrase here and there: Hit-and-run. Delaware. Identified.

"Our baby's gone!" Maureen cried. "She's gone!"

Maureen sobbed without speaking. Uncle Keith continued to hold her. Abby glanced at him, and wondered what he'd do or say, given that he already knew and yet couldn't tell Maureen. Abby saw a tear slide down Uncle Keith's cheek. She wished she could say something to him, and also say something to Maureen. But despite their gifts, there was nothing that she or Uncle Keith could do. All they could do was know about terrible news before everyone else.

CHAPTER 14

Abby and Uncle Keith painted the bathroom in silence. They hadn't spoken on the drive home from the wharf. Abby knew he needed some quiet time after comforting Claire's mother. She would've been fine reading in her room if Uncle Keith hadn't suggested they go ahead and paint the bathroom. "We should try and do something productive, at least," he'd said with the smallest smile possible to still call it one.

Abby could tell, though, that Uncle Keith's heart wasn't in the task at hand. Neither was hers. Seeing Maureen sob while knowing she couldn't say anything, that she had to act like she hadn't known already while trying to think of the best way to understand how it felt to lose someone—it was all too much, and it weighed so heavy that the fruit of Abby and Uncle Keith's labors were a few errant lines of white over the ugly wintergreen color, like jagged lines of white-out added in a rush over a document.

Abby set down her brush and looked at Uncle Keith. He held his roller aloft, but it stayed still. He stared at the wall with sad eyes and cheeks gone ashen with sorrow.

"I'm sorry about Claire," Abby said. "And Maureen, and—just everything."

"Me too," Uncle Keith replied with a sigh. He set down the roller and shook his head. "I wish I could've stopped her."

"You tried."

"Not hard enough."

"Claire dying wasn't your fault."

"And I have to pretend I first heard the news from Maureen, that I didn't already know she was dead, that Claire told me she was running away in the first place, and how she was running away from Max. I'm just so tired of keeping secrets, Skipper. I couldn't tell anyone about the things I see, and now I can't tell anyone about something else. It sucks." He smacked the wall, then cursed as he pulled away his hand, which now had a streak of fresh paint on it.

"I wish I knew how to help," Abby said.

"It's not your problem to fix," Uncle Keith said as he rinsed off his hand.

Seeing the paint run down his palm reminded Abby of Betsy's stained hand in her office. "Can I talk to you about what I saw in the bookstore?" Abby asked.

"Oh, right. Yeah, sure." Uncle Keith shook his hand dry and turned to face Abby.

"So, I talked to Betsy a bit, in her office."

"Ah, that's where you disappeared to."

"I went to her office because I saw blood coming from her door." Uncle Keith raised his eyebrows. "It was coming from a whistle on her desk. Mary's whistle."

"Oh, she talked to you about Mary?" Uncle Keith paled. "You didn't tell her you could see her, did you?"

"No. She knew that I knew about the murders, but that was it."

"Ah, okay. Good. I don't know how she'd react to that. She's—well, you can't talk to her about Mary."

"She told me she thinks she's innocent."

Uncle Keith nodded. "She's a nice woman, but that's one thing where she won't see reason."

"We see dead people and you're commenting on her lack of reason?" Abby smiled, and Uncle Keith chuckled.

"We may be crazy, but—well, Betsy isn't crazy, she's in denial. She won't accept the evidence. And before you ask, the evidence is all there. Fingerprints, behavior—"

"I know, I know. But the only thing I wanted to tell you was that, when she held the whistle, the blood from it spilled over her hands and her skin started to curl like Mary's does. And then I saw a word: 'stained.'"

"Stained?"

"Yeah. It was all over her hand, like scars."

"Stained." Uncle Keith checked for paint, then leaned against the wall. "Stained, stained—with what?"

"I don't know. Have you ever seen words on people?"

"Never. The most I've seen is Mary slowly flaying on the beach. Scared the shit out of me the first time I saw it. I try to avoid her now."

Abby shuddered at the memory of Mary's ghost unraveling into bloody threads.

"Well, whatever it means, it looks like you got something extra with everything you can see."

"Yeah." Abby just wished she knew why—and further, what it all meant.

Abby and Uncle Keith were eating breakfast the next morning and talking about what to do that day when a knock at the door interrupted them. Abby and Uncle Keith both looked towards the hallway. "You expecting someone?" Abby asked. She hoped it wasn't Chloe coming over.

"No," Uncle Keith said as he got up. Abby followed him and wondered who it could be. Would it be Maureen with more news about Claire, news that Uncle Keith would have to act his way through again? Was it the cops? Abby paled at the thought. Surely they'd have no reason to be back, not with Claire found and Uncle Keith being nowhere near her.

Abby shook her head. She also realized it'd been a couple days since her head had been filled with so many swirling questions. They'd calmed considerably when she realized she could confide in her uncle.

Uncle Keith froze when he opened the door. "David! What are you doing here?"

Abby's eyes widened, and she approached Uncle Keith's side. Her father and mother were standing on the porch. Abby's stomach fell faster than an anchor into the ocean. Her parents couldn't be here already.

"I'm not supposed to leave until Sunday," Abby blurted.

Her father gave a half smile. "What, no, 'Good morning Dad, I'm not supposed to leave until—'"

"We had a change of plans," her mother interrupted. Abby tried not to look at her mother with the same hatred she felt creeping through her body. Her mother hadn't wanted her to come up in the first place. She was certain her mother was the reason they were here early. "We figured we'd come up, visit real quick, and then bring Abby home."

"Why?" Abby cried as Uncle Keith, to her dismay, stepped aside to let her parents come inside. "I'm having fun here."

"What, fun fixing up the house?" her father asked. He looked around the living room as they stood in the foyer. "It looks the same as when we dropped Abby off. Haven't you done anything, Keith?"

"We painted the bathroom," Abby said. "And Uncle Keith's been working all week, which you kept saying you wanted him to do, right?"

"Abigail." Her mother gave her a sharp look, but it was Uncle Keith's pained look that made Abby feel guilty. "Don't talk to your father like that."

"David, Denise," Uncle Keith said. "What's going on? Is something wrong?"

"Why don't you tell us?" Abby's father said. His small smile remained, but his eyes began to change. Abby's hatred mixed with fear in her stomach.

Uncle Keith furrowed his brow. "About what?"

"We saw an interesting story in the news this morning. Who's Claire Baxter?"

Uncle Keith's eyes narrowed, but before he could answer, Abby asked, "How did you hear about Claire?"

Both of her parents looked at her with wide eyes, and Abby felt brief satisfaction at catching them off-guard. "How did *you* hear about Claire?" her mother asked.

"From Carmen—but first, from Uncle Keith." It took all of Abby's strength to not puff out her chest in satisfaction.

Uncle Keith cast a warning glance at Abby, one that told her not to interject further. Abby felt herself wilt like a rose under a sudden burst of rain. How could he push her out of the conversation, like her parents had done so much before, when she was trying to defend him?

"Claire was my student," Uncle Keith said.

"Yeah, we know that," her father spat. "Now, anyway."

"What else did the story tell you, so you don't interrupt me with everything you already know?" Uncle Keith snapped back.

Abby's father fumed, and her mother added in a cold voice, "They said you'd been under investigation in relation to her disappearance."

"And did they say I was involved?"

"No."

"And I haven't been in Delaware at all this summer, so I definitely wasn't involved with her being hit by a car." Uncle Keith's voice was choked, and Abby thought of how he'd broken down when he told her about seeing Claire's ghost. She wanted to hug him, but figured that would only upset her parents; which increased her venom for them tenfold.

"We didn't say you were involved."

"Then why are—"

"Because you didn't tell us anything!" her father exploded. He threw up his hands and stepped towards Uncle Keith. Abby feared her father would hit him, but her father dropped his hands back down. "How could you leave out the fact that you were under a goddamn criminal investigation before we sent our daughter to stay with you?"

"I wasn't under an investigation! They asked me questions and let me go. The cops haven't spoken to me since. Everything else is just media hype."

"They said you used to meet with her a lot," her mother said. "How much were you involved with this girl?"

"She was my student and she was part of an after-school reading program I do with the kids. She was with me at the diner before she disappeared because we were meeting as part of that program."

"At a diner?" her father asked. "Are you serious? Did you even think about how that would look?"

"It was Claire's idea, and we got permission to meet there from her both of her mothers, one of whom was friends with Sandra."

"Why couldn't you meet at the school like the other kids?" her mother asked.

"Because her boyfriend kept coming by and bothering them," Abby said.

"Abby, please," Uncle Keith said. "I've got this."

Abby stepped back and shut her mouth. She tried to replace the feelings of hurt with feelings of hatred, which made her feel stronger.

"Abby's right," Uncle Keith continued. "Max kept harassing Claire at our meetings, and it was interfering with our work. Did they talk about that in the story, or did they just talk about what a monster I am for being a teacher who gives a shit?"

"They only asked Max how he felt," her mother muttered.

"I'm sure he felt a lot of things," Uncle Keith said. "I hope he felt like the sack of shit he is for making Claire run away in the first place."

"How do you know all this?"

"Claire told me. She entrusted me before she left, and she was going to tell me when she was safe so I could tell her parents." Uncle Keith sighed and looked at the ground. "But then … well …"

Her mother's face softened, and Abby felt her own anger begin to crack.

"You still should've said something to us," her father said.

Abby glared at her father. He didn't notice. He was too busy boring holes into Uncle Keith, who looked up with sullen eyes. "You should've explained all this before we sent our daughter up here, so we wouldn't have to see it on the news."

"I didn't think it'd be on the news—"

"And you should've told Claire's parents the minute she ran away."

"I couldn't do that. Cynthia is friends with Max's father, the whole town loves that family—"

"You really think Claire's mother would choose her friend over her daughter?"

"Claire thought so. She thought that Max would talk his way out of blame. That's why she wanted to get away first, before she told them."

Uncle Keith's voice broke as he spoke, and for the first time, Abby began to doubt his reasoning. She tried to keep it down, refusing to side with her father's irrational anger. But she couldn't help but wonder how irrational it really was.

"But you're not Claire, Keith," her father said. "You're her teacher, and a damn adult. You're supposed to do the thinking for her, not do her bidding; especially when she's just a scared teenage girl."

"I tried to stop her from running away."

"How? By asking nicely? By hoping things will just work out if you do what everyone says and go with the flow? It doesn't work like that. It didn't work with Sandra—"

"Sandra has nothing to do with this," Uncle Keith said through clenched teeth.

"And it didn't work with Claire, obviously."

"I know I fucked up, David! You think I don't feel like a rat bastard every day? I felt like I was going to betray Claire if I broke my promise, and I found out very quickly that it didn't even fucking matter. She was dead."

"Yeah Keith, she's dead! This isn't something me or our parents or anyone can fix for you!"

"Oh, like you or Mom and Dad ever fucking fixed anything for me!"

"SHUT UP!" Abby screamed before she could stop herself. Her father and uncle looked at her with shock, but all she saw was the way they'd been before: her father an angry and belligerent brother, her uncle a timid man who made terrible decisions and couldn't admit to them without making excuses. She hated feeling that way about two people she loved, and in that moment, she hated that she loved them.

"Just stop!" she said. "I fucking hate this!"

"Abby," her father said, "Don't say the f-word."

"Really, David?" her mother snapped.

Abby felt a flash of gratitude, but it didn't last. It wouldn't last as long as she stayed in the house, submerged under years of anger between her father and uncle.

Abby stormed towards the door. "Abby!" Uncle Keith called. She ignored him as she ran outside and slammed the door behind her. She had to get away—not far, and not forever, but just away. She ran towards the shore and down the beach, then slowed her pace when she reached the dock.

Abby watched the ocean, and tried to calm herself by breathing in time with the waves. She braced herself for her mother or father to come after her.

No sound came. Abby only heard the ocean. Her shoulders relaxed.

Abby sighed as her father and uncle's argument replayed itself in her mind. A breeze went through her hair and clothes, and Abby wrapped her arms around herself to keep warm. She turned, ready to walk slowly on the beach to clear her head.

Someone stood behind her.

Abby froze.

Mary stood in silence. Her skin began to flay, and blood seeped from the torn cracks.

Abby stayed still. She asked, "Do you want to talk to me?"

CHAPTER 15

Mary turned away from Abby. Abby almost screamed in frustration, until Mary lowered herself and sat on the dock. She patted the spot next to her.

Abby sat down beside her. Blood dripped from Mary's ankles into the sea. Abby kept her feet on the dock.

"You know you're bleeding, right?" Abby asked.

"Of course I do." Mary's voice was a whisper and a song all at once. Abby heard it with her ears, and yet it seemed like an echo heard first in her mind.

"You just don't seem too bothered by it."

"I've been like this ever since I died." The sea rolled against the pillars of the dock. Mary's voice seemed to roll with it, moving in and out of Abby's ears like a current, and disappearing in time with the hush of the waves. "It's my mark."

"How did you get it? You weren't flayed when you died."

"No. The flaying came after. It's to tell the dead what I am."

"That you're hurt?"

"I am, but that's not what my wounds are telling them. Look at me."

Abby didn't want to watch Mary fall apart in front of her. Abby almost regretted hearing her speak. Mary's voice echoed through her like her own thoughts, and it chilled her more deeply than the presence of the dead ever did.

"Please look at me," Mary said. "You can see me, and you haven't run away. I want someone who understands to see me."

Abby felt Mary's plea in her heart. It was, after all, what Abby had wanted when she began to see the things she never wanted to see.

She turned her head towards Mary.

Mary stayed intact. She faced Abby, her expression monotone. Her skin blew like tendrils in the sea breeze, which made her look like a calm, peaceful monster. Abby saw neither muscle nor bone, but rather a shadow of where Mary's skin had been. The blood that seeped through her swirled and moved across that shadow, but not at random. All across Mary's body, Abby saw a single word spell itself out over and over again: MURDERER.

"This is why they won't speak to me," Mary said as she motioned towards the blood.

"Who?"

"The dead. They see what I am."

"So you *are* a murderer. You killed those kids."

Mary nodded. Abby felt a surge of revulsion course through her body. "Why?" she asked.

"I was afraid. I could see the dead, like you. They floated in and out of the trees, appeared in my path and looked through my window. But they wouldn't speak to me. I figured they were warning me, letting me know they would get all of us soon if they couldn't have some of us. They didn't ignore me, but I was certain there was a barrier I needed to break in order to protect everyone."

"That's no reason to kill people. That's the complete opposite of protecting them."

"I know."

"Would've been nice if you knew that before."

"And now I'm being punished. Trust me, you can't say anything to me I haven't lived with since my death. I don't expect you to feel sorry for me, but I hope you'll listen and understand."

Abby looked out over the water and fumed.

"I'm punished with the mark of someone who brought people to the realm of the dead before their time," Mary continued. "Murderers like me, murderers that the dead know from our marks to hate and revile."

"Yeah, I get it, you killed four kids and now you have something to show for it. What do you need me for? You want me to pass on an apology for you? Those kids won't talk to me either. None of the dead will."

"I know they won't. It's because you're like me."

Abby snapped her gaze back to Mary. "What do you mean?"

"You look like I do to the dead."

Abby's mouth dropped, but then her anger returned. "I'm not like you," she said. "I haven't killed anyone."

"But someone close to you has. Look."

Mary reached for Abby. Abby recoiled, but Mary still held her hand in the air between them.

"Don't you want to understand?" Mary asked. "Isn't that what you want: for people to tell you things?"

Abby glared at Mary. She wondered how much Mary had been listening to her and her uncle all week. Still, Mary had a point: Abby had wanted answers, and Abby had wanted people to listen. She'd also wanted someone to talk to. Uncle Keith had been that person, but quickly shed that role the moment her father had walked in the door. Mary was here. Mary didn't want to push her away.

Abby held out her hand. Mary took it. It felt like ocean spray upon her palm. Mary grazed her thumb along Abby's palm, and a smear of blood was left behind. The blood disappeared with Mary's touch, but not before Abby saw STAINED glaring up from her skin.

Mary ran her hand up Abby's arm. Abby's skin began to flay and curl like Mary's, though she felt no pain. Blood covered her forearm, and STAINED curled across her arm in swirls and wisps. Abby gasped and jerked back her arm. The blood and curlicues of skin disappeared along with the words, but Abby still held her arm close to her chest.

"You look like I do to the dead," Mary said. "It's a different word, but it's the same warning, the same sense of revulsion—"

"I look like your aunt," Abby said, as she remembered Betsy's bloodstained hand in the bookstore.

"Aunt Betsy," Mary said with a sigh. Her words disappeared into the wind, and Abby felt their chill run down her spine. "My mother's sister."

"Yeah, that's usually what an aunt is."

"That's your answer."

"That Betsy's your aunt? I fucking knew that!" It was bad enough Abby found out she was stained somehow, but Mary talking to her in some mystic riddle bullshit was too much.

"No. That it's something in the blood."

"What, the word?"

"No. Your blood. You're stained by a blood relative. Aunt Betsy is my mother's sister. My mother will be stained as well. But Uncle Todd—Betsy's husband—won't be."

Abby felt the coldness settle on her body like frost upon a windshield. "Uncle Keith is my blood relative," she whispered.

"He's not your only one. The only rule is a direct bloodline. It could be—"

"How do you know these rules?" Abby narrowed her eyes, partly in hopes to keep the tears that began to sting them inside where they belonged. "Do you get some stupid guidebook or something about all the things the dead can see?"

"No. I heard about it from those like me, those who are stained with the blood we spilled."

"And their relatives, I guess."

"No. That's shed upon death. We only see it on the living."

"What? Why? That makes no sense."

"Life makes no sense. But it's a stain that goes away once you shed a life that's filled with questions." Mary's hand settled on Abby's again. Her whisper was so cold and close, it echoed in her head. "Imagine a life without questions, a life without the stain of your family."

Abby closed her eyes and felt her thoughts quiet for the first time in weeks. She only heard Mary's voice and the waves of the ocean.

"Imagine all of it washing away," Mary purred. "Wouldn't you just love to dive in?"

The ocean sounded as soothing as Mary's voice. Abby wondered how calming it would be to let the ocean fill her ears, to do nothing but listen to the sea, just like Uncle Keith's boat proclaimed.

Abby stirred at the thought of Uncle Keith. She felt the misty sensation on her palm, tiny waves that felt like fingers as Mary tightened her hold.

"Let the ocean protect you," Mary whispered. "Let me protect you, just like I protected them."

Abby's eyes snapped open. Her gaze fell on the water, where Mary's blood swirled in the foam that lapped against the dock. The blood and foam swirled into a word of its own: RUN.

She jerked away from Mary and jumped to her feet. Mary looked at her with a vacant smile, MURDERER curling in and out around her lips.

"No," Abby said. "Stay away from me and Uncle Keith. Stay away from all of us."

Abby stormed off, and hoped that Mary would stay behind. When she was close to the house, she looked behind her. Mary still sat on the dock, but she was simply a shadow that flickered in time with the waves.

―――――

Abby shivered at the memory of Mary's words. She felt confident that Mary wouldn't come to her again, but that didn't stop the things she'd said from echoing in her mind. Mary was stained with the mark of a murderer. Abby was marked as well by association. But who was she associated with?

Mary had seen Uncle Keith before, at least according to Uncle Keith. Mary hadn't said it was him, and deep down, Abby knew she had no reason to believe Uncle Keith would be marked. He hadn't driven the car that hit Claire. He hadn't forced her to run away. Claire dying wasn't his fault, just like Laura dying wasn't his fault. After all she'd done to assure him of that, the least she could do was believe it herself.

All she knew was that a blood relative had passed on the stain. That could be anyone. It could be her parents, but Abby almost laughed aloud at the thought. Maybe her grandparents. Abby raised her eyebrows in thought. Her father hated his parents, and even Uncle Keith had called her grandfather an abusive asshole. Maybe he'd been a murderous asshole.

Abby looked at the house, hesitant to go back inside. She didn't want to walk in on her father and Uncle Keith arguing, and she also didn't want to be taken home. It was encouraging that no one had come to retrieve her. Maybe they'd decided she could stay, that Uncle Keith was innocent.

Was he, though?

Abby shook her head. He was.

But who wasn't?

Abby's gaze floated down to the sand in the front of the house. The trails of blood she saw when she first arrived ran towards the driveway, steady and quick. She figured they were coming from the basement. They were lines only she could see. If she wanted answers to her questions, she'd have to go to their source.

Abby strode into the house. The door smacked closed behind her. Her mother, sitting in an easy chair by the window, jumped at the sound. Abby didn't see her father or uncle. She wondered briefly if they'd killed each other, and smirked at the thought of that being the reason for her stained hands.

She knew it wasn't, though; and while she didn't know if the basement had the answers she was looking for, she knew it'd be as good a place as any to start.

"Abby," her mother said, with no raised voice nor trace of anger. "Do you want to talk, sweetheart?"

She didn't, and even if she did, she had no time to pause. She walked by her mother and through the hall. In her periphery, she saw Uncle Keith and her father at the kitchen table, both of them with beers in hand despite the hour. *Like brother like brother*, she thought with an eye roll as she continued on.

"Abby?" she heard Uncle Keith call. She ignored him. Chairs scraped against the linoleum, and footsteps followed behind her.

"Abby," her father said. "Come and talk to us, honey. Uncle Keith explained—"

Abby reached the basement door and jerked it open. She didn't want to stop and speak. She was afraid that if she stopped to hear about how everything was right again, that she'd lose her courage to go into the basement and find out what was wrong.

"Abby!" Her father's voice was closer now, and she heard several pairs of footsteps follow her down the stairs. She heard them more than she heard the hisses and growls of Felicity and the other campers, all of whom scattered to the walls as Abby walked by them. She saw one box in the stack of many begin to bleed, even as Felicity stayed in the corner.

"Abigail, I know you're mad at us," her father continued. "But you still need to show us some respect when we talk to you."

"I'll talk to you in a minute," Abby said as she reached for the bleeding box.

"You'll talk to us now." Her father grabbed her shoulder and tried to pull her away. Abby shook him off, and he grabbed her with a stronger grip. "Now!"

"Abby, listen to your father," her mother said.

"What do you want that box for?" Uncle Keith asked.

Abby turned and gave him a pleading look. "This box is different from the others," she said, hoping he'd understand what she meant. She didn't want to say what she really saw in front of her parents. She knew they wouldn't believe her. "I want to see why," she added. "Please."

"What's different?" her mother asked. "It's the same as the others."

"Why do you care what's in there?" her father asked, eyes still narrow.

"Why don't you let her find out?" Uncle Keith asked. Abby's father snapped his gaze to Uncle Keith, but softened when he saw that Uncle Keith's expression had no malice. "Obviously it's important to her."

Her father sighed. Uncle Keith took the moment her father looked away to wink at Abby. Abby felt relief in her heart for the first time that morning. She pulled out the box and brushed off the dust.

"Here."

Abby looked up and saw her father holding out a set of keys. "You can use it to rip the tape," he said.

Abby nodded in thanks, then ripped through the tape and opened the lid.

Other than the familiar smell of must, she was greeted by a yellow Sangway Bluff Middle School sweater, a baseball, and a framed picture of a Red Sox player.

"Jesus. My old Nomar photo," her father said as he picked it up.

"Are these your things?" Abby asked as she looked in the box for the source of the blood. She saw no blood except on the side of the box. It seemed to be coming from the middle, so she began to dig.

"Looks like it," her father said. He knelt down and picked up the sweater.

"That always looked terrible on you," Uncle Keith said.

"Why do you think it's buried in this box?" her father said. They both laughed, and it was pleasant to hear after all the screaming they'd done earlier. Abby smiled to herself, even with her bloodied errand.

After a few moments of digging, Abby saw a teal shoebox with "KEEP OUT" written in Sharpie across the top. Blood seeped from its corners.

The warning and four yellowed pieces of Scotch tape were all that was in place in terms of security. Abby sliced through the tape easily with her fingernail. In the box was a faded photo of Felicity and a younger version of her father standing on the docks near her grandparents' house. There was also a gold locket that bled profusely into the cardboard.

Abby lifted the locket from the box, and blood spilled over her hands. It wasn't as jarring a sight as when Mary had touched her, but she still shivered a little as STAINED made itself clear on her skin.

"What's that?" her mother asked. Her father and Uncle Keith were still examining the sweater and the photo. Abby's mother took the locket. The blood vanished from Abby's hand, and while Abby could see it swirl over the band of the necklace and the locket itself, her mother's hand stayed clean. "Fe-li-ci-ty," her mother read slowly. Her mother snapped her mouth shut, eyes wide with recognition. Abby realized her mother must know about Felicity, and wondered for a moment how neither of them had told her anything about it.

Uncle Keith and her father stopped speaking and turned to face her mother. "Where did you find that?" her father asked.

"I did," Abby said. "It was in a shoebox with a photo of you and Felicity."

Her father looked like he'd been slapped. "You know about Felicity?" he asked. "How?"

"David," her mother began as she touched his shoulder.

"How?" her father repeated, ignoring her mother.

"I—I read about her in a book," Abby stammered.

"I told her," Uncle Keith said.

Abby looked at Uncle Keith, as did her father; though his expression was much more furious. "What did you tell her?"

"She asked me about my job, and when I told her about Claire being gone and all the media surrounding that, the Blueberry Island murders came up."

"Jesus, Keith, why? You didn't have to mention this, she never had to know—"

"Why not?" Abby asked. "It's our history."

"It isn't. It's something that happened, it's something that's over, and it's something that happened because a crazy teenage girl couldn't let go of the dead."

"Then why did you keep her stuff?"

Her father pursed his lips and fumed. Abby tried to keep her bravery, but felt like a child again beneath his anger.

"I have that locket," her father said, "because Felicity left it with me the night before she died. She didn't want to lose it in the woods, before her campout with Mary, and—" He swallowed, sniffed, then grabbed the locket from her mother's hand and held it with a clenched fist. "I put it in that box along with that photo so both could be kept out of sight. So both could be buried right along with her."

"But you didn't bury it," Uncle Keith said.

"Really, Keith? Not now."

"You kept it. A part of you wanted to remember her."

"I wasn't going to just throw it away. I'm not a monster."

"What's the harm in telling Abby about all this? What harm has it done you for her to know? It can't be worse than everything you've felt by keeping it all buried."

Her father closed his eyes and took a deep breath. He opened them, then looked at Abby. He furrowed his brow when he looked at her. "What?" he asked.

Abby didn't answer. She was transfixed by his hands. Blood seeped from the locket to his fingers, knuckles, and wrists. In clear and perfect view, MURDERER swirled across her father's skin.

CHAPTER 16

"What's wrong, Abby?" Her father held out his free hand. Abby flinched before she could stop herself. His expression darkened, then returned to normal.

"I'm not upset anymore," her father said. "Well, not as much. I'm sorry I grabbed your shoulder. I shouldn't have done that. No one should grab you, okay?"

It was impossible. How could her father be a murderer? The same man who'd told her bedtime stories, who sang to her when cleaning up her cuts and scrapes so she'd ignore the sting, who'd pleaded with her with frightened eyes to forget she'd seen the girl from the Legend of Locker 751—

Abby's thoughts froze in their tracks. She glanced at Uncle Keith's middle school yearbook, which lay on top of another box.

"Abby, is something up?" Uncle Keith asked. "Something else different about the box, or—"

"Different?" her father asked. "What do you—"

"Dad, who was the Girl in Locker 751?"

Both Uncle Keith and her father looked at her. "She never had a name," her mother said. "She was just a ghost story."

"And she wasn't real," Uncle Keith said.

"Thank God you know that," her father added.

"She wasn't real, Dad?"

"No. Sweetheart, I told you, she was just a fake character in a story."

"You didn't tell me that."

"What?"

Abby felt tears prick at her eyes. She hoped the dim lights in the basement hid them from her father's view. She glanced at the ghosts with their backs turned and seething against the wall. She thought of Laura crouched in Locker 751, banging her head against the metal. She thought of everything she'd seen that her father said wasn't there—but in the end, he'd told her a lie about someone who never existed, and it was to cover up the truth about what she'd seen.

"You told me she was real," Abby said as she swallowed down what felt like pieces of her breaking heart swimming up into her throat. "You told me there'd been a girl who really was murdered and stuffed in the locker—"

"I meant that was the story." Her father's voice cracked a little as he spoke, but to Abby, it sounded like a chasm.

"You said there were stories *about* her, but that she was real, she existed."

"She didn't, Abby," Uncle Keith said. "Your father's right."

"But he told me that, and told me the real girl had gouged her eyes out too—"

"*You* told her that?" Uncle Keith spun to face her father, who looked at his feet. "You, the one who'd always tell me ghost stories weren't worth telling? What the hell?"

"He wasn't telling me a ghost story, though," Abby said. She stormed over to the other stack of boxes and grabbed the yearbook from the top. "He didn't want me to think I'd seen *her*." Abby opened the yearbook and held up Laura Pennington's photo.

Her mother and father looked at the yearbook with startled faces. "What do you mean?" her mother asked.

"This is who I saw in Locker 751. This is who was banging her head against the locker, who snarled at me and had gouged-out eyes. Dad said Laura did it to imitate the original girl, a story he told me was the truth, even if what I saw was a lie." Abby slammed the book down. "Which is it, Dad? What's the lie, and who's telling it?"

"Abby," her mother warned.

"Tell me! I want to know what the hell I saw!"

"Abigail!"

"Stop!"

Her father's voice silenced both of them. Abby looked at her father and saw a man who looked much more defeated than the tone of his voice had suggested.

He set the locket down, then placed his fingertips upon the yearbook with his free hand. He closed his eyes and drew a shaky breath. His next words were a whisper, but they rang in Abby's ears as clearly as a scream.

"I didn't mean to."

Everything was quiet in the basement, save for the sounds of the dead children breathing in the corner. They glared at them, but thankfully didn't roar or scream. Still, Abby and Uncle Keith ignored them. They instead stared at Abby's father alongside her mother.

"David," her mother said, her voice a choked whisper. "What do you—"

"Didn't mean to what?" Uncle Keith said. His voice, however, was at a normal tone. It was also upset enough to tell Abby that Uncle Keith knew exactly what.

Her father looked up at Uncle Keith. The sadness, grief, and guilt on his face was so devastating that for a few moments, Abby forgot that he'd admitted to murdering a young girl. "I didn't want to," he began.

"Want to what?" Uncle Keith spat. "Tell us."

"He has," Abby said. She pressed her lips shut, startled by her act of pity towards her father.

"I want to hear it," Uncle Keith said, though he still appeared to speak to David instead of her. "I want him to say it clearly."

"Can one of you please just tell me what's going on?" Abby's mother asked. "How does Abby know about all this?"

"She's the girl I saw in the locker," Abby said. "The day that I got scared. The day you picked me up from school."

"The one you thought you saw?"

"She did see her," Uncle Keith said. Both Abby and her mother looked at Uncle Keith in shock, but Abby's was combined with gratitude. "I believe her, especially because she described seeing things that only applied to Laura. She had Locker 751 when she died."

"And Laura was convinced that that stupid ghost in the legend was living in there," David said. "She had Keith convinced, and it looks like Keith's convincing Abby too."

"I didn't say anything to Abby until she told me what she saw," Uncle Keith said. "And I didn't believe Laura. I knew there was no girl in there."

"Then why were you going to join her for that stupid séance?"

"Because I wanted to help her. She was just a scared girl with an overactive imagination."

"And that's exactly what Mary was! They were the damn same: people who took the stories they heard and the things they imagined and made them so real, they were dangerous."

"Laura wasn't dangerous."

"She was! I overheard you guys enough to know why you were friends, and I remember how you'd try and tell me people could see the dead. They can't, Keith; and when they're like Mary, they kill innocent people so they can create actual dead people to see."

"I know what Mary did, but everyone isn't Mary. I wasn't going to end up like Felicity and the other kids. I wanted to talk her down from what she thought she was seeing."

"Right. All it would've taken was fifteen minutes and she'd have had you convinced the Girl in Locker 751 was real."

"She wouldn't have. I knew there wasn't anyone there because *I* couldn't see anyone. I saw a teacher who died in a car accident every day in the science lab—"

"You didn't."

"I saw an angry kid who lurked around the cafeteria—"

"I've seen him too!" Abby said, remembering the rude boy she'd almost collided with at lunch.

"You didn't!" Her father's yell made Abby jump. He looked at her with wild eyes and a reddening throat. "There was nothing there, and you need to stop thinking you saw—"

"That I saw what you believed I saw long enough to lie to me?" Abby yelled back.

Her father leaned against the boxes and clenched his fists.

"It doesn't matter if you think I saw something or not," Abby said. "What made you hurt Laura?"

Her father took a deep breath, and then another. Both she and Uncle Keith stayed quiet, not wanting to push her father away from telling the truth.

"I didn't want Felicity to go that night," her father began. "She told me how Mary was going to take her and the other campers on a ghost hunt. She thought it sounded cool, that Mary was going to tell them her best stories and scare all of them. Mary always rubbed me the wrong way, but I thought it was just Mom and Dad rubbing off on me."

"What'd your parents have to do with it?" Abby asked.

"They never liked the ghost stories our town told."

"They never liked anything resembling imagination," Uncle Keith added with a snort. "Inspired too many emotions—as in any."

"And in this case, they were right," Abby's father said. "I didn't say anything to Felicity, though, because I didn't want my parents' words to take away from Felicity having fun. I thought maybe they were wrong."

"They were wrong," Abby said, as she remembered the cold smile on Mary's face when she'd attempted to coax Abby into suicide. "There was more wrong with Mary than believing in ghosts. Lots of people believe in ghosts, and they don't all go around killing people."

"Well, Mary did, and killed my girlfriend and three of my friends," her father said. "All I could think about afterward was what would've happened differently if I'd spoken up, if I'd tried harder to keep Felicity from going, if the camp had done more to keep Mary in line instead of encouraging her imagination. She needed to be told no."

"So you told Laura no instead," Uncle Keith said with narrow eyes.

"I went to talk to her to protect you, Keith."

Her father looked at him with sad and pleading eyes, but Uncle Keith was not mollified. "You didn't just talk to her."

"That was the plan. I went to the school that night to tell her to leave you alone and to stop telling stories. When I got there, though, she looked terrified—"

"Yeah, because my seventeen-year-old brother showed up instead of me, and ready to bite her head off."

"She had some weird cloth out and a rock on a string—"

"That was her pendulum. She thought she could use it to talk to spirits, like a Ouija board."

"Was she a witch?" Abby asked.

"No. She just dabbled in occult shit, especially when she was desperate."

"So was her knife just dabbling?" her father asked.

Abby's eyes widened, but Uncle Keith seemed unfazed. "Her penknife?"

"The silver one she was twirling when I got there."

"It was her grandmother's. She thought it was her connection to the spirit world. Again, dabbling, and again, bullshit."

"Well, when I saw that knife, all I could see was Felicity's throat."

Abby saw Felicity lift her head as she looked towards David. Her throat began to bleed.

"I saw Laura doing to you what Mary did to Felicity, and I—I just …"

Uncle Keith folded his arms, and Abby's mother put her face in her palm. Abby thought she saw a tear slide down her mother's cheek. All four of the dead children narrowed their eyes as blood trickled from their bodies to the floor.

"I couldn't see anyone except Mary," her father said in a quiet voice. "I couldn't feel anything except all the rage, the confusion, and the anger I'd been trying so hard to keep inside, like Mom and Dad wanted me to. I couldn't do anything except yell, and when Laura cried and tried to insist the girl was real, I kept seeing Mary's intense stare as she told stories; and when Laura held her knife towards me, I grabbed it and—and I just wanted to stop the staring. I just wanted her to stop seeing things that meant the people I love would get killed."

Abby's stomach curled, and Abby's mother muffled a sob into her hand.

"And I kept slamming her into the locker, trying to rid myself of Mary, of Felicity, of all the memories I had because everyone around me couldn't stop seeing things."

Abby thought of Laura slamming her face into the back of the locker over and over again. It was a clanging she'd never forget, and now, she had the image of her father's hand holding Laura's head in place while it happened.

Uncle Keith sniffed, and spoke in a choked and cold tone. "How'd it get labeled as a suicide?"

"Dad," Abby's father said.

Uncle Keith snorted again and turned away. "Of course."

"What'd your dad have to do with it?" Abby asked to either Uncle Keith or her father, whoever would answer.

"Dad was a sheriff, remember?" her father said.

"And friends with the coroner and full of influence in the department," Uncle Keith added. "Good ol' Sheriff Gillman, a shady cop and a shit father. Of course he'd get his son off for murder."

"It was an accident—"

Uncle Keith spun around and punched Abby's father all in one swoop. Her father stumbled back and held his nose as blood spilled over his knuckles.

"Accidents are when you trip and fall," Uncle Keith spat. "They're when you drop a glass and it breaks. They're—"

"They're when you tell a teenage girl you'll be her cover for her when she runs away?" her father spat through a mouthful of blood.

Uncle Keith wrestled Abby's father to the floor and punched him in the jaw. Her father protected his face but otherwise made little movement to defend himself. Abby ran towards them, but her mother interfered before she could reach them. She pulled her back and moved away from her father and uncle.

Abby's first instinct had been to protect them—either Uncle Keith or her father, she didn't know, even with everything her father had confessed. It was a confusion she couldn't reckon with, couldn't understand. She understood, though, that her mother's first instinct was to protect her daughter.

Her father didn't seem much interested in protecting himself. Uncle Keith punched him several times, then placed his clenched fists on her father's chest. He lowered his head, and Abby head him crying. Abby's father reached up to Uncle Keith's arm, but when he touched him, Uncle Keith shook him off. He crawled over Abby's father and sat against the wall opposite the four dead children, sobbing into his fists. Her father sat upright and stared at the floor.

Abby glanced over at the wall, where the dead children were still huddled. She wondered if her father's confession, apologies, and grief had done anything to change their behavior. She wondered if they at least would look at her or Uncle Keith, who'd done nothing except share a bloodline with her father, with less revulsion than they had before.

Felicity and the other children glared at Abby. They stood in silence for a moment, then let out the same growl she'd heard before. The growls because a scream like wind, one that sliced through the rain of her uncle's tears.

Abby's mother squeezed her shoulder. "Let's go upstairs, honey," she whispered.

Abby wondered briefly if it'd be a good idea to leave her uncle and father alone with each other, but knew it wasn't on her to decide. She took her mother's hand as they both left the basement.

CHAPTER 17

The sounds of Uncle Keith's sobs and the dead children's roars quieted behind Abby as she and her mother walked up the stairs. Everything around Abby felt muffled and numb. Her head was like cotton and her skin felt like it was covered by a worn, scratchy blanket that she couldn't shake off.

Once they were away from the basement door, Abby's mother broke away from her. She crumpled onto the couch and began to sob. Abby stood and stared, feeling helpless as she watched her mother fall apart in front of her. Abby had no idea what to say or do. How could Abby talk to her about how her husband had killed someone? How could Abby talk about what she'd learned about her father?

Abby's face crumpled. She swallowed, then turned out of the room, leaving her mother alone to cry. She went upstairs and entered her room, closing the door behind her. Brigsby smiled at her from the bedside table.

Abby grabbed Brigsby and threw him against the wall. He bounced to the floor and stared up at her with the same smile and the same golden eyes. Abby dropped onto the bed and folded into herself. She didn't want to think about her father's crimes or her uncle's troubles. She didn't want to think about anyone in her family. She didn't want to feel anything. She didn't want to see anything new. She wanted everything about that week to disappear into the ocean and turn to foam against the shore.

Abby's phone rang. Her first thought was to fling it against the wall alongside Brigsby, but her better judgment peeked through just enough to prevent that from happening. She looked at the screen and saw that it was Carmen.

Abby ignored the call. She didn't want to talk to Carmen and have someone else know the degree to just how fucked up her family really was. She could try to keep it hidden, but she also knew that neither her mood nor her voice were in any shape to keep her secrets for her.

The ringing stopped. Her phone chimed with a text almost immediately after. *Hey, you're coming home tomorrow, right?* Carmen asked.

Abby tapped her reply in a blur: *Don't know*. Abby realized this was true. Where would they go? Would her father come with them? Would they all stay here?

Carmen wrote back, *Why not? Something happen?*

Abby was about to lie, but found her thumb hovering over her phone instead of typing that everything was fine. She sighed a little, then wrote, *Yes but I don't want to talk about it.*

She felt a different sort of regret when she hit send. She wished she hadn't said she didn't want to talk about it. She found herself wanting to talk to someone, someone who wasn't her family and yet someone who was always willing to listen. There was a comfort in knowing there was someone she could confide in that wasn't a relative, and until that moment, it was a comfort she hadn't realized she needed so much.

Before Abby could backtrack, Carmen replied, *Okay, hope everything's alright. Talk to me whenever and lmk when ur home.* It was followed by a string of heart emojis and two girls hugging, but it was the words that made Abby smile.

"Abby."

Abby looked up in mild surprise at her mother, who stood in the doorway with puffy eyes.

"Pack your things," her mother said. "We're going home."

Abby felt the return of the questions she'd thought of before, namely whether or not her father was coming. Something told her not to ask in that moment, though. She got off the bed without a word and grabbed her suitcase.

Abby brought her suitcase downstairs and saw her mother by the door. Neither her father nor her uncle were in sight.

"You ready?" her mother asked as she nodded towards the door.

Abby was about to step forward, when instead, she glanced back towards the hallway leading to the basement door.

"Did you tell them we're leaving?" Abby asked.

"They'll figure it out."

Abby felt the sadness and anger in her heart melt into an ache. She didn't want to leave Uncle Keith alone and sobbing. She didn't know what her father would do without them there.

"Abby."

Abby turned towards her mother with a heavy heart. Her mother looked at her with pity and kindness, which Abby wasn't expecting.

"Uncle Keith will be fine," her mother said. "As fine as he can be, anyway. It's something he needs to sort out himself, or at least with his brother. It's certainly not on his niece to sort it out for him."

Abby was about to protest being removed from the issue yet again. She'd already learned so much about her family, more than she ever wanted to know. How could it get worse? Why couldn't she be involved in their healing?

Her mother's face, though, was different than Abby had ever seen it. It was weary and defeated instead of frustrated. Abby felt the need to argue dissipate into sadness. She didn't have a choice in the matter. She was too young to have one. She felt like she always would be.

Abby swallowed a small lump in her throat. "I just wish I could help," she said.

"I know you do, sweetheart." Her mother walked towards her and put a hand on her shoulder. "But staying here will do none of us any good. You can call him later, okay? He'll be alright."

Abby wasn't sure about that, but she did believe her mother that leaving was the only thing they could do. She pulled her suitcase behind her and they walked out of the house.

They drove in silence, punctured only by an occasional sigh from her mother. Abby didn't watch the coast as they left it behind. She didn't want to see Blueberry Island or the wharf. She didn't want reminders of the week she'd had and the lifetime she'd learned about in those few days. The learning that came from seeing the ghost of a dead girl in an abandoned locker.

Abby's cheeks grew hot. She remembered Uncle Keith crying at the table and saying that their shared gift only brought him pain and grief. Abby understood exactly how he felt. All she'd seen were ghosts from her family's shared pasts, wounds that wouldn't heal and sins their bloodline would never be forgiven for.

Abby's shoulders fell as she thought of the unwavering glare of the children in her uncle's basement. Her innocence didn't matter. Her father's guilt and sorrow didn't matter. None of it mattered to the dead, because confessions and apologies did nothing to change the fact that they were dead. It didn't change the fact that her father had killed someone, or that she and her uncle were stained. Seeing the dead changed none of these facts, either—it just made them easier for Abby to uncover, to give her grief, confusion, and anger a place to settle. She supposed that was better than having to bury it all, but keeping her secrets with the dead wasn't much help when they wouldn't listen.

Even when they weren't angry, though, they were ambivalent—Uncle Keith had said as much when he said the dead ignored him. Mary said the same. Abby supposed it wasn't the dead's job to speak to them about the things the living couldn't understand. Maybe the fact that she saw them was just a fluke, something that was a part of her the way some people sang with perfect pitch or hated the taste of bell peppers. Maybe it was all part of a bigger mess, one that no one could really clean up, even if they tried.

The thought of everything being an uncleanable mess, one that she couldn't be a part of fixing, provided Abby with a surprising sense of peace. She'd been so angered by her parents and Uncle Keith leaving her out of things because she thought they thought she wasn't ready for answers. Maybe the truth was that their own answers were merely questions, things they didn't know and couldn't pretend to for the sake of their daughter.

Abby looked at her mother. Her mother stared ahead with red eyes, but no tears fell from them.

"Mom?"

Her mother looked at her and gave her a sad smile. "Yes?"

Despite her relative peace with not knowing, one question gnawed at her. It was one she had to at least ask, even if no good answer came. "What's going to happen with Dad?"

"I don't know."

Abby looked at the dashboard. It was the same answer Abby had when she asked herself that question. Her father had never hurt her. He'd also killed a girl in cold blood. Did the fact that her father felt guilty about it make it any less bad? And whether or not it did, did it mean it was okay for her to love him?

"And I wish I did," her mother continued.

Abby looked at her mother. Her mother added, "I wish it was easy for me to tell you that I'm definitely going to leave him, that we're definitely going to move on, that I can draw that line between right and wrong, but—"

"But you can't," Abby said.

"No." Her mother's voice began to sound choked, and she swallowed. "No, I can't—not without lying to you. And I don't want to lie to you, Abby, even if it means you see me for who I am."

Abby touched her mother's elbow. "It's okay, Mom. I love who I see."

Her mother let out a sob, one she quickly swallowed down. With one hand, she patted Abby's knee. "I love you too, honey," she said. "I always will. And—and so does your father. He—"

"He's with Uncle Keith. We can talk to him—well, about him tomorrow."

"Yeah. Yeah, and don't feel like you have to talk to him just because he's your father."

"I won't. But I don't know if I will or not. I have to think about it."

"Think about it as long as you want. Even if it's a lifetime."

Abby thought of never talking to her father again, and her heart ached. She thought of Laura's ghost bleeding and broken in Locker 751, and the thought of never talking to him again ached a little less.

"Slightly changing subjects, though," her mother said. "What were you and Uncle Keith talking about, when you said you both could see something?"

Abby hesitated, remembering the swiftness of adults, save for Uncle Keith, to not believe her. However, most of the truth had already been shared in the basement. Abby needed to learn to trust what she saw and to assert it out loud, even if everyone didn't believe it. The best way to learn was to practice.

"Uncle Keith and I can see the dead," Abby said. "When I saw a girl in Locker 751, I saw Laura. I've seen a kid in the cafeteria, kids in Uncle Keith's basement—"

"While we were down there?"

"Yes. I've seen a teenager on the beach, and Mayor Holden."

"Mayor Holden? That old mayor from the 1900s or whatever?"

"Yeah. He was an asshole—he flipped me off."

Her mother laughed, and though it held a hint of the sadness she'd had before, it made Abby smile. "I guess seeing the dead doesn't mean they'll be nice to you," she said.

"Nope. None of them are. It's—" Abby thought better of bringing up her father again. "They don't want to," she said.

"Hm. Same with the living, I'm afraid." Her mother squeezed Abby's thigh. "Don't focus on them, though. Focus on the people who do want to talk. People like me, and your uncle."

"And Carmen," Abby added, thinking of her text messages earlier.

"Yeah. It's something you'll need to remind yourself of from time to time, probably for the rest of your life; but it's good to remember."

"I'll try." Another thing Abby learned about growing up was realizing that was all anyone could do.

Acknowledgments

I'm sitting down to write this after many days of procrastination. I'm filled with gratitude, gratitude I want to express for those I'm going to acknowledge. But finding the will to sit down and write it all out has been a challenge, to say the least.

It's appropriate that I've felt this way about writing the acknowledgments for *Seeing Things*, because that state of mind describes how I wrote this book. I wrote the story in my smallest chunks to date for a full-length book, usually 300-500 words a day if I was feeling productive. Those productive days often felt like pulling my own teeth to get the book done. It's my shortest book and yet the one that took the longest to write.

Still, it was written, which is ultimately what matters. I'm glad it was written, because it was based on an idea I've had since before my first novel was published. In my old neighborhood, I often saw an old man walking up and down the sidewalk, stooped in his step, and never noticed by anyone else walking by. While I knew they could see him without acknowledging it, my imagination started to play around—what if no one else *could* see him?

From there I got an idea for a young girl who could see the dead, but only realizes this when she sees someone walking by that her friend can't see. She then sees that same man in an obituary in the next day's newspaper. Dun dun DUN! But when she tries to talk to him, he scowls and runs off; and when she corners him, he tells her in less-than-polite terms to buzz off.

I had my hook: she can see the dead, but none of them want to talk to her. But where to go from there? The short story I began was focused on her learning more about her abilities, meeting a fellow psychic who was also an English teacher, and then the two of them realizing that the girl's inability to let go of a death in her past was keeping spirits from leaving this mortal plane. That death was her dog's, and the story ended with a really sad scene of the girl letting her dog's spirit go near the pond where they used to play.

I felt like something was missing, and set the story aside. I finished *The Crow's Gift* and *Please Give*, then wrote *Wither*, *Without Condition*, and *Little Paranoias: Stories*. This little story stayed in my mind through it all, but it was when *Little Paranoias* was out for edits that I got an idea: what if the fellow psychic is the girl's uncle? What if instead of being unable to let go, they both share a mark that repulses the dead? And what if the greater story is a history of murder and lies that the girl's gift brings to the surface?

I finally had my story—and it became a novel. A novel that through all my slowness, got finished; and one that's now in your hands.

It always takes me a while to realize the small miracle that is a book's completion, but it doesn't take me long to recognize everyone who helped me see the book through. Evelyn Duffy, my amazing editor, helped me keep the story alive by listening to me talk about it in our earliest meetings. She listened to the first full treatment (the one with the dog) and seemed okay with it, then offered invaluable guidance and feedback when I saw it through to its final form. Working with her motivates me to build on ideas and not give up on the ones that just won't quit. And it almost goes without saying this next bit, but I want to say it because I'm thankful for it: her edits, feedback, revisions, and notes helped make my manuscript even better. Thank you, Evelyn, for your amazing work.

I also want to thank Doug Puller for his amazing cover art, and for formatting the book. I'm always awed by Doug's talent, and feel incredibly lucky to have been able to work with him for all of my books thus far.

Thanks to Norm Miller and Violet Castro for being the book's first readers. They both provided excellent feedback and encouragement. Norm also helped me with the technicalities of crime reporting. Thank you both!

Thanks so much to everyone who's read my work, shared it online, reviewed it, and encouraged me; especially when I'm getting anxious about it. The horror community is so supportive and includes some of the nicest people you'll ever meet, especially my fellow women in horror!

Thanks, as always, to my mom and dad. This book has less sex (as in none), so, you're welcome. Sorry for all the darkness, though. And the language. Love you both.

And as always, many thanks to my wonderful husband. I love you, Will. Thank you for your support and encouragement.

Thanks for reading, everyone. Stay healthy and safe.

Photo by Karen Papadales

About the Author

Sonora Taylor is the author of several short stories and novels, including *Wither and Other Stories*, *Without Condition*, and *Little Paranoias: Stories*. Her short story, "Hearts are Just 'Likes,'" was published in Camden Park Press's *Quoth the Raven*, an anthology of stories and poems that put a contemporary twist on the works of Edgar Allan Poe. Taylor's short stories frequently appear in "The Sirens Call." Her work has also appeared in "Frozen Wavelets," "Mercurial Stories," "Tales to Terrify," and the "Ladies of Horror Fiction Podcast." She lives in Arlington, Virginia, with her husband.

Visit Sonora online at sonorawrites.com.